BACK STABBER

J.H. WEAR

Pre- Covid time period.
To my friend Gary Dorn. Live long and prosper.
Maybe this dedication will convince you to buy me a beer at the local pub.

Note: This story takes place pre-Covid. So, there were no masks, restaurants were fully open, and people were not worried about keeping a hockey stick's length away.

In the story, I mentioned Canadian Tire money. They gave these paper monies out at Canadian Tire during a purchase, in nominations of five cents to two dollars. I believe they are now discontinued, but at one time several retailers accepted Canadian Tire Money.

This is the third book of the murder mystery series with Detectives Anya Roberts and Moss Stone; following A Taste Of Murder and Play Dead. Roberts and Stone have a close relationship, partly because they dated before they became partners as detectives.

CAST OF CHARACTERS

Ryan Morgan - Married to Brooke Morgan
Brooke Morgan - Married to Ryan Morgan
Joseph McCarthy - Married to Rachael McCarthy
Rachael McCarthy - Married to Joseph McCarthy
Rover Driscoll - Married to Lydia Driscoll
Lydia Driscoll - Married to Rover Driscoll
Paige Butler - Best friends with Brooke Morgan and Michael Sutton
Michael Sutton - Friends with Paige Butler, former boyfriend of Brooke Morgan
Melisa Regan - secretary to Ryan Morgan
Moss Stone-Senior detective
Anya Roberts - Stone's detective partner. Roberts and Stone dated before becoming partners.
Cindy Stiegel - Stone's girlfriend

1

Friday, August 3, 2018

BROOKE MORGAN STOOD, WATCHING THE PARTY THROUGH THE OPEN PATIO doors as she wiped the marble counter around the sink. She dropped the cloth into one of the double sinks. One knee was bent, tilting her hips. She checked again if anyone was watching through the patio doors.

"It looks like the party is going well." Michael Sutton spoke from her side.

"Yes, and drinks do help make a party." She placed her hand on his resting on her hip, and slowly pushed it off. "Someone may see."

"Not from there."

"Everyone can figure out we're the only ones in the kitchen. Come on, let's join the others." She shook her long blonde hair and walked to the patio, her heels making a clicking noise on the ceramic tan and grey kitchen tiles. It did not surprise her Michael Sutton had followed her to the kitchen, especially since she wore stressed blue jean shorts and a cropped red top. His hand on her hip was pleasant, but it was also dangerous if anyone saw them. As she stepped through the open French doors, she saw her husband close the white steel lid of the barbeque as smoke filtered out. Ryan Morgan wiped a hand on the blue apron that covered a checkered green and white short-sleeve shirt and tan shorts.

"How are those steaks looking?" Brooke noticed a beer sitting at a side table that held cooking utensils and sauce. She passed him the beer and placed a hand on the back of the medium-built man. Ryan was average height with dark hair, with his Italian heritage coming through on a handsome face.

"Looking good. Five minutes for medium-rare." He took a drink from his can of beer.

"Okay, I'll bring out the rest of the food." She turned back toward the house, giving a wave to Paige Butler for her to follow her.

"What's up?"

"Help me carry out stuff."

"Sure." She joined her at the kitchen table, picking up a bowl of potato salad. She gave Brooke a small hip check. "We should have a girls' night out next weekend."

Brooke laughed. "Too soon. Even Ryan would start wondering about our friendship." Ryan knew Paige was a lesbian, and he had pressured Brooke for a three-some when they were first married. Brooke convinced him she was only interested in men, and Paige was only a friend. After a period, he gave up on the idea of the three sharing a bed. She glanced at the raven-haired, athletic woman, admiring her abs. Paige liked to wear strong colours that complimented her copper-coloured skin. Today she wore black shorts and a green bikini top.

"I thought he was just worried about men after you."

"Yes, well, and I want to keep that speculation to a minimum." She carried the Caesar salad in one arm, and the plastic plates in another.

Paige followed Brooke to the outside table, placing the bowls at the centre. She whispered, "Is there a particular guy I can speculate on who has a lusty attitude for you?"

Brooke raised an eyebrow at her and went back to the house as Paige giggled.

———

RYAN TOOK A DRINK AND COMMENTED TO MICHAEL SUTTON AND ROVER Driscoll as they stood by a glass topped patio table. "One thing you can say about summer. It sure makes fashion more interesting." He glanced over at the women setting out food. Most wore shorts and summer tops, although Rachel McCarthy wore a back-less yellow bathing suit and dark blue shorts. Lydia Driscoll was conservatively dressed in longer shorts and a short-sleeved top.

Rover frowned. The bearded man was heavyset and peered down at Ryan. "One shouldn't lust after other women. Remember, you're married to Brooke."

"Cut the crap. I'm just looking. If women want to show some skin, who am I to keep my eyes away?"

"One of those ladies is my wife." He squared his shoulders, straining his grey golf shirt.

Michael was almost Rover's height, but slimmer. He kept his brown hair short, that revealed a small scar on his forehead. His striped shirt showed off a muscular chest. He placed a hand on Rover's chest. "Hey, let it go. Ryan is just spouting off." He looked across the patio with three identical tables on the wood deck. The cedar deck covered only a portion of the treed backyard. He watched Brooke take a platter of steaks from the barbeque area to a table covered with a tablecloth.

Ryan and Rover glared at each other as Brooke called out, "The food is all set on the table. Time to eat."

Rover stepped in front of Ryan and headed toward the food.

Ryan shook his head and smirked. "I guess he didn't get that big by being last at the food line."

Michael replied, "Keep it down. This is supposed to be a fun get together."

"Jesus, you nag me like my wife."

———

PAIGE SAT ACROSS FROM MICHAEL AT ONE OF THE PATIO TABLES. "I GUESS we're the odd couple here. Both unmarried and living the free life."

He laughed. "Yeah, and we're both chasing women."

Paige grinned. "But I'll bet I'm more successful at it."

"Ouch. I suspect you are. At least I'm not having much luck."

"What happened to Lisa? You were going with her last time I saw you."

"Ah, she wasn't my type."

Paige tilted her head. "Not your type? She was a blonde, if I recall. Like all your previous girlfriends."

Michael took a drink of his beer. "What about you? What's your latest pursuit?"

Paige shrugged and took a bite of her steak. "A lady doesn't tell. Besides, I've an advantage. If I get lonely, I can always revert to men."

"I remember." He chuckled.

"Those times are hard to forget." She laughed. "Our triangle, as we used to call it."

"How are the steaks?" Ryan walked up to their table and stood with a cooler and a can of beer, placing them on the table.

"Wonderful. Everything is great," Paige answered first.

"You have a talent with the barbeque," Michael agreed.

After Ryan walked away, he lowered his voice. "Have you heard any rumours about Ryan?"

"No, why?"

"Just stuff I heard, and he was bragging about the money he was making."

"Come on, spill, what do you know?" She leaned forward.

"It seems our friend is making a nice side income from a bar he owns. Unreported income."

"How do you know this?"

"Later. Let's join the party." He gave a nod toward the kitchen, where a few guests had gathered. He stood and waited for her to stand. Michael put an arm around her waist, giving her a brief hug. "Let's talk later, maybe where we can't be overheard." He went to the kitchen, giving a grin at Brooke. "Splendid party, but where are you hiding the booze?"

Brooke laughed and pointed at a portable bar across the kitchen. "You don't normally have any trouble figuring out where the liquor is."

"True, but you're a distraction." He made his way to the bar.

Paige looked at his departing back and returned her attention to Brooke, who raised her eyebrows. Paige smiled and gave her a short wave with her fingers. She proceeded to where Rover was holding a can of ginger ale. Next to him, his wife Lydia was surveying the living room.

"How are you and Lydia doing? I heard you were doing a lot of work at the church."

"It's rewarding work." Lydia gave her a squeeze on her hand. "We're fixing up the church yard so we can have more outdoor services and add a play area for the children. How have you been keeping?"

"Good, busy with my training classes." She was pleased. Even as Lydia became more involved with the church, she stayed in contact with her. It was harder to read what Rover thought of her. He had a hard look to him, which she considered wasn't surprising since he had spent time in prison for assault with a weapon.

"That's good. It certainly keeps you in shape. Rover and I must have you over for dinner soon."

"That would be nice."

"Let's try to set up something before summer disappears." Rover added one of his infrequent comments. A smile almost appeared before it evaporated to his normal reserved look.

"Sure." Paige knew he was reserved to most people. Lydia told Paige once he believed people still judged him for his time in prison. "Talk later. I think I'll get a refill." Paige went toward the bar, noticing Ryan chatting with Joseph and Rachel, pointing his finger at them as if he was giving a lecture.

———

MICHAEL TOUCHED HIS CAN OF BEER AGAINST THE WINE GLASS BROOKE WAS holding. "Delightful party. You did a great job preparing the food." He looked around the living room where music played. The guests had retreated inside after dark clouds rolled above.

"Don't forget Ryan cooked the steaks."

"Yeah, he reminded us of that earlier." He glanced at the dining room where Ryan was conversing with Rachel and Joseph McCarthy. "But you're the reason I love coming over here."

She sighed. "I know. But I don't need complications in my life. I'm married to Ryan, and that's how it is."

He saw the flash of lightning through the windows. Seconds later, the rumble of thunder caused everyone to pause. "Fuck, he doesn't deserve you."

"Thanks, but being married to him will not change anytime soon." She placed a hand on his arm. "Find a girl that you like who isn't committed to someone else. I better mingle."

Paige moved to join Brooke as she made her way across the living room. "He has that lusty attitude. No surprise there."

"Hush."

"I know you. It's not having an affair with him that scares you. You don't want to hurt him. Again."

"Stop analysing me and my situation." She smiled. "Even if you are right."

Brooke looked into the living room, watching Joseph walk over to the table with snacks. He attacked the nibbles on the dining room table as if he had missed dinner, while Rachel continued a quiet conversation with Ryan. She saw Rachel nod as he spoke, her eyes paying full attention to him.

"Excuse me, I need to talk to Ryan. She crossed the dining area, where the large black oak table held drinks and food, and proceeded along the hardwood floor to where Ryan was standing.

"Hi, everything okay?" She glanced at Rachel, who retreated a half-step.

"Of course. I was just telling Rachel about our trip to New York last month and how vibrant the city is." Ryan touched Brooke's arm.

"You can reminiscence about New York later. We need more beer and wine for our guests."

Brooke watched Ryan walk away and turned her attention to Rachel. "So, Joseph and you are planning a trip to New York?"

She shook her head. "No, I wish." She stared at Joseph, still working on potato chips. "Joe can't take time off work right now."

"I should help Ryan with the refreshments." She returned to the kitchen, opening the pantry door to retrieve another bag of potato chips.

"What's up?" Paige approached her.

"Nothing, other than my husband flirting with another woman." She sighed. "What does Rachel see in Joe? She's standing by herself, and all he does is eat chips. He's got to be the dullest man in the country."

"Different strokes for different folks."

"And you certainly know about different strokes."

2

Friday Evening

DETECTIVE ANYA ROBERTS PARKED HER CAR AT THE BACK OF THE downtown shopping strip. A sign warned parking was for customers' use only and security cameras were present. She locked her car, making sure nothing was visible to any would be thieves. On the other side of the parking lot, stood the Local Bar and Eatery. She made her way to the front entrance, seeing her reflection as she went past the glass-walled patio. The image showed a slim, tall brunette with short hair, her height accented by her high heels.

Just beyond the sign informing customers to seat themselves, she saw fellow detective Moss Stone and his girlfriend, Cindy Stiegel. She took a deep breath. *I hope this doesn't turn awkward.*

Moss Stone, tall, lean and with naturally curly hair, stood as Anya Roberts approached the high-top table. "Anya, this is Cindy." He gestured to the pretty blonde.

"Pleased to meet you." She shook her hand. Anya hoped she and Cindy could fool Stone that this was the first time they met.

"Good to meet you as well. So, you're the poor woman detective who has to accompany Moss on his work."

"It has its moments. Moss has a different way of solving crimes." Anya laughed.

"I'll bet." Cindy touched Moss's arm. "See if you can catch the server's attention."

Anya asked, "What do you do for excitement? Moss told me you work in a bar."

"Yeah, the Craft Beer Market. That's part-time work. I go to university, play the guitar and do photography."

The server, a tattooed brunette, arrived to take their drink and food order, momentarily halting their conversation. When she left, Anya commented, "Wow, that must keep you pretty busy. And you date Moss on top of all that."

Cindy smiled. "Dating Moss is the fun part, although it's not always easy to get together."

"What type of photography do you do?"

"A little of everything. I'm taking a photography course and we get different assignments." She grinned. "Moss was a model in one of them."

"Do tell."

"No, not another word." Moss held up his hands.

"Okay, okay." Cindy laughed.

"A change of subject is in order." Moss looked at Anya. "How was your meeting with Tanya Conner?" He spoke to Cindy. "Tanya was the girlfriend of the actor that was murdered."

"Oh, Paul Church. Yes, I remember reading about that." She glanced at Anya.

"It was tough, though I think she'll be able to move on. She's going to the funeral in Calgary, which will help give closure." Anya took a drink of her gin and tonic. "The saddest thing was he was murdered just because two other actors were bored and wanted to create chaos in someone's life."

Stone reached for a chicken wing. "Yeah, murder should involve some passion or reason for it."

Cindy used her figure tips to comb back her long, blonde hair. "Passion is good for a lot of things." She watched him gulp down his beer. "I guess I'll be driving." She reached for his car keys sitting on the table.

"It's a standard."

"I can handle a stick." She grinned.

"Don't start talking dirty. My colleague has a very pure nature."

"Since when?" Anya smirked.

Stone signalled the server for another beer. "I'll be back in a minute."

Anya watched him leave. "Okay, so far, he doesn't suspect we met before. Let's be careful what we say. He doesn't miss much."

"I know. He's smart even when he's drunk."

"Tell me about those photos."

"I took nude photos of him. Tastefully done, kind of artsy."

"How in the world did you convince Mr. Private to do that?"

"I told him my photography course assignments comprised nude photography. If he didn't want to pose for me, then there were plenty of my other male friends who would. So he agreed."

"Very clever to appeal to his jealous side."

"I suppose so. But actually, it wasn't part of the assignment at all." She grinned. "I tricked him."

Anya covered her mouth as she laughed.

"Sometime maybe I'll show them to you. Just don't ever say anything to him about it."

"I won't. I'm happy he's found someone like you. He was dating a lot of women before he met you."

"I guessed that." Cindy paused and took a drink. "He admitted he went out with you before."

"A long time ago, before we ended up in the same police department and as partners. We're just friends now."

Moss returned. "I'm still hungry. How does nachos sound?"

Anya commented, "That would be good. You should slow down on your drinking, otherwise we'll have to carry you out of here."

"Good point. Maybe I'll switch to coffee after this beer."

Cindy smiled. "Yes, you and your coffee. The stronger, the better."

Moss gave her a curious look. "What can I say? I like good beer and good coffee."

3

August 5, Sunday Morning

MICHAEL STARED OUT THE PASSENGER WINDOW OF THE MERCEDES SEDAN, observing the tree-lined private road to the golf course. The asphalt road was smooth but narrow, with signs urging caution, and a posted speed limit lower than practical.

"How's work going?"

"Too well. I'm having to spend evenings working. Good money, but a lot of extra hours," Ryan retorted.

"Look, it may be none of my business, but I hope you're not doing anything illegal. You're not desperate for money. Don't risk what you have just for more of it."

"What can I say? I'm on a roll. I just have to work the mine a while longer."

"Fair enough." He looked in the front part of the centre console, noticing a receipt that appeared ready to fall to the floor mat. He picked it up and rescued it. "Do you want this?"

Ryan glanced over. "Yeah, parking receipts are a tax deduction."

Michael looked at the slip of paper before restoring it to the centre console, the print showing it was a valet parking receipt from the downtown Marriott Hotel. "It's good you still have time for golf and other endeavours."

"That I do." He chuckled. "Some activities are more pleasant than others."

Michael twisted to look at Ryan, but he said nothing until he parked his car.

"Looks like a great day to golf." Ryan passed a golf bag to Michael and took out his own from the trunk. "I see Joseph and Rover are already here." He pointed at the white Ford pickup truck.

Michael looked at the big truck that Rover used for work. It also did extra duty for hunting and pulling a holiday trailer. "That truck has seen its share of back roads and bush. Did you hear about the time when he shot that moose last year?"

"No. What happened?"

"After he shot the moose, he cleaned it out using this massive hunting knife before loading it onto the truck. He used his hands and just that knife to gut out that moose. For a church goer, he sure has a less than passive side in him."

"Yeah, remember he spent time in jail for assault." Ryan shrugged.

"I guess it's a good thing he met Lydia," Michael replied. "He doesn't seem to get into any trouble. Heck, he only has one beer on our golf days."

"I suppose so. Lydia is one woman I do not find attractive. Gossips, goes to church five days a week, and gives the evil eye to anyone who has more than two drinks."

"She has her beliefs. She has always been nice to me."

They passed the clubhouse, a two-story building designed for dining and banquets, proceeding to a second building that housed the golf carts and a golf store. They saw Joseph and Rover had already signed out two carts.

Joseph made a show of looking at his watch. "You guys slept in?"

"Ryan drives like an old lady. The golf cart may be more to his speed." Michael laughed.

"Says the guy who wanted to stop at Tim Horton's for a coffee on the way here." Ryan dropped his golf bag into the back of the cart. "Shall we do the usual bet? Losers buy lunch."

"Sure." Joseph pointed at Michael. "Want to take on these misfits?"

Ryan held up his hand. "Whoa. If you're taking Michael, then Rover and I want a handicap of three strokes."

"Whatever." Joseph looked at Michael. "Let's see if we can put your new putter to good use."

The two golf carts rolled past the third hole. Michael nudged Joseph as they stood watching Ryan prepare to tee off.

"He's a good golfer, but sometimes forgets to count all his strokes."

Joseph nodded. "Golf isn't the only thing he bends the rules at."

"What do you mean?"

Joseph lowered his voice. "Rover told me he made a mistake of investing a good chuck of money in one of his properties, a bar, a while back."

"What happened?" Michael watched the ball sail into the distance.

"From what Rover told me, he lost money and Ryan has made money. Go figure. Ryan's accounting method. Rover said if he lost much more, there'll be hell to pay. And we all know about Rover's temper." He walked toward the tee.

Joseph addressed the ball and his follow through sent the ball high and toward the green of the fourth hole.

"Nice hit." Michael placed his ball on a tee.

"Thanks. I just imagined the golf ball as Ryan's head and gave it a good whack."

"Whatever works."

4

Thursday Evening

PAIGE BUTLER GIGGLED AS SHE SAT WITH BROOKE MORGAN AT A TABLE near a window. The lounge was crowded with the two women getting several look overs from the male dominated bar. "I'm telling you, that guy in the green shirt is undressing you with his eyes."

Brooke did up the top button on her blouse. "Why didn't you tell me the button was undone before?"

"I thought you had left it open on purpose. You know, trying to seduce me." She grinned from the side of the square table they shared.

"Right. Me trying to seduce you. I thought it was the other way around. I'm married, remember?"

"When you have an affair with another woman, it's not really cheating." She took a drink of her white wine. "Just saying."

"That's rather strange logic." Brooke glanced around the bar again. The man in the green shirt was still observing her. She considered him rather good-looking, wearing the urban-cowboy style well.

"Maybe. But it's true." She twisted around to see what Brooke was looking at. "Ah, Mr. Green Shirt is still interested even after you did up the top button. Want to drive him crazy?"

She shook her head. "No, I don't." She took a drink of her wine. "What were you going to suggest? Undo two buttons?"

"That would work too. But how about if I lean over and give you a kiss? Nothing drives men crazier than two women kissing."

"No, no, no. Let's keep that aspect of our relationship a secret."

"Come on, it'll be good for a laugh. I'll kiss you, and you just watch how he reacts."

"Paige, you mustn't." She grinned and wagged a finger at her.

"I'll take that as a dare." She shifted in her chair and pulled at Brooke's arm. "If you resist me, I'll get up and sit on your lap."

"Oh, shit, you're serious." Brooke flipped her hair back and leaned forward, kissing Paige on the lips. "Okay, that's it for public affection." She looked at the green shirt man, who stared back slack-jaw.

"Come on, admit that was fun. It took you out of your comfort zone."

"Okay, it was fun. But if word ever got back to Ryan, it would be tough to explain."

"What? That two girls exchanged a kiss. How is that news?"

"Yes, well, Ryan is not exactly a calm, understanding male. I told him you were just a friend, and I was only interested in men."

"I suppose it's good he believes that." Paige laughed. "I have to say he doesn't exactly ooze being monogamous."

"I know, I know. Ryan is what he is. I knew why I was marrying him."

"That was a difficult time for all of us. A lot of tears then and later."

Brooke stayed silent and lowered her head.

"I'm sorry. This isn't the time or place to bring that up."

Brooke frowned. "I thought he'd change after we got married. Our group, we've all known each other for a long time. I was hoping Michael, or even Rover, would help him be more responsible."

"You can tell Michael is still in love with you."

"More like lust. No, I made a choice. I was really stupid that summer and it changed everything. I betrayed our triangle. But this is now. I can't live looking at a rear-view mirror. There're some issues I have with Ryan, but every couple goes through difficult times. I'm hoping he'll understand that money isn't everything."

Paige reached over and held Brooke's hand. "Just stay who you are. Don't worry what he does."

"Thanks."

"Now undo that top button and let's go to my place."

"Why undo the top button?"

"A goodbye present to Mr. Green Shirt. He'll appreciate the gesture."

She grinned and undid the top button. Brooke stood and left with Paige, holding her hand as they reached the lounge exit.

They crossed the parking lot to Paige's Jeep, a white four-door Wrangler.

Brooke closed the passenger door and did up her seatbelt. "I like your Jeep, but the ride is uncomfortable."

"I know, but I didn't buy it for physical comfort. I had a Volkswagen before. Good gas milage, but when trucks saw me on the road, it was like they felt they could run me over. With this," she patted the steering wheel, "they give me space. I'm a single woman and I need to feel secure when I go out."

"The Jeep does that, I suppose."

"That and I know kick boxing. Also, take a look in the glove box."

Brooke opened the glove box, revealing the owners' manual, assorted papers, and a knife. "Is that in case you come across the steak that needs cutting?"

"It's good to be prepared for emergencies. I wasn't thinking of steaks when I bought the knife."

"Be careful. I don't want to hear of you getting cut by that knife. That's a dangerous weapon."

"I know how to use it, and it's only for last resorts."

Brooke closed the glove box. "Enough about weapons. Let's go to your place and enjoy the evening."

5

Tuesday Afternoon

PAIGE BUTLER CLOSED THE DOOR TO HER JEEP AND PEERED AT THE SIX-story building. The building was on the west-end of downtown. She was familiar with the area. Across the street was Charmaine's Coffee Emporium, one of her favourite spots to go to for coffee. Their pastries were made daily and usually sold out by late afternoon. With a sigh, she made her way to the front entrance of the building. The glass doors admitted her to the lobby and the elevators, where she pressed the call button. When the elevator doors opened, she pressed the third-floor button.

Office three-one-zero featured a dark wood door advertising R. Morgan Commercial Reality. Paige stepped inside and waited for the young, dark-haired secretary to acknowledge her. The secretary closed the book she was reading with a sigh.

Paige noticed the manicured figurenails, the carefully applied makeup and the expensive blouse she was wearing. She resisted frowning. Despite her looks, Paige found her unappealing. A desk plaque read Melisa Regan.

"I have an appointment with Ryan Morgan."

"One moment."

She stepped from her desk, showing off a short skirt and long legs. She tapped on a second frosted glass door before entering. "Ryan, you have a visitor." She turned and looked at Paige. "What's your name?"

"Paige Butler." She snapped out the reply.

"Send her in," Morgan's voice called out.

Melisa beckoned Paige to enter, scrutinizing her as she stepped by.

Paige ignored her, closed the door, and sat in one of the leather-covered chairs facing the desk.

"So, what was with this strange text message you sent me? Asking me to see you at your office concerning a personal opportunity. What kind of shit are you trying to pull now?"

Ryan sat behind his desk and gave a smirk. "I'm trying to help you and help my business."

"This better be good." She crossed her arms and her legs.

He laughed. "It'll be good for me, regardless. There's a client that's flying in next week for a dinner meeting. I need to conclude a business transaction, one that will give me a healthy commission. I want you to attend the dinner with me as my associate. A pretty girl like you will help finish the deal."

"Why would I help you? If you want a pretty girl to help you, you know a lot of other women who could be your pretend work associate."

"My client is a woman. She likes women. Flirt with her enough so she wants to do business with me."

"Why would I agree to being an escort to help you, of all people?"

"Two reasons. I'll give you five hundred bucks."

She grunted. "What's the other reason?"

"I won't show these to anyone else." He swung around the computer monitor on his desk and touch the keyboard.

Paige sat shocked, staring at the nude images of herself. "Fuck. How did you get those?"

"Exactly." He chuckled. "I remember many years ago you hinted you made some money doing model work. It was when you were a poor student and needed cash. You wouldn't say exactly what modeling you did, but I did some research and figured out who the photographer was. I bought the pictures."

"You must be some kind of a jerk to get those."

He turned the monitor to face himself. "Very nice photos."

"What the fuck are you going to do with them?"

"Nothing. That is, if you help me secure that contract."

"If I help you, will you delete those pictures?"

"We'll see. Right now, they're our secret. Dinner is for Monday evening at the Double Tree hotel on Mayfield Road. Wear something nice." He turned his chair and went to the safe next to his desk. "I'm going to give you the monetary incentive."

She watched the heavy black door of the safe open and saw stacks of white mailing envelops bulging with rubber bands securing them closed. Ryan opened one envelope and pulled out several bills. He closed the safe door and stood, offering fifty and one hundred-dollar bills to her. "Five-hundred dollars for one night's work."

"I will not sleep with her."

"I'm not asking you to. Just be nice and do some flirting. That's all I need."

Paige stuffed the money into her purse. "So, why didn't you just offer me the money and see if I'd take the job? Why show me those photos at all?"

"Just so that you know I have them. It's in case I run into a situation where I need your help right away."

"I won't forget this garbage you're pulling. Karma can be a bitch. You better watch your fucking back." She stood.

Ryan shrugged. "Look, it just happens you're the only lesbian I know. Well, at least one that has a secret that I know of. I need your help. I've had these photos a long time, just so you know I can keep a secret."

"You're still a prick." She walked out of the office, slamming the door behind her.

A few moments later, the secretary opened the door, putting her hands on her hips as she stood in the doorway.

"What did she want?"

Ryan smirked. "She wanted to cover her ass." He elaborated. "Just a business transaction she wasn't happy to accept."

"Whatever. Are we still on for drinks?"

"Sure, I'll tell the wife I'll be working late."

6

August 9, Thursday Afternoon

Ryan looked up from his desk when the door opened, revealing his secretary. "Yes, Melisa, what is it?"

"A guy from Hi-Lite Bar is here. It isn't Mitch." She shrugged. "He said his name was Tyler."

"Damn. Send him in." He watched as Melisa used her hand to wave at someone in the adjoining room and stepped to the side.

A skinny man with a scruffy beard entered the room. He looked to be in his thirties and cast an anxious look around the office. "Uh, Mitch asked me to give you this." He produced a white, sealed mailing envelope with rubber bands around it from inside his leather jacket. The coat looked worn, with the logo of the University of Alberta on it.

Ryan tapped on his desk. "Leave it on here." He watched as the man surveyed the office and dropped the envelope on the desk. Tyler minded him of someone who did too many drugs, but there was intelligence in the way in he looked around the office. He didn't trust him. "Okay, you can go."

Melisa looked behind her and swung her attention back to Ryan. "Different deliveryman this time."

"Yeah, I need to speak to Mitch about that. I want him to make the delivery himself." He picked up the envelope, opened it, and looked inside. "Looks good." He rolled his chair a few feet to the side of the desk to a black safe sitting on the floor. Ryan turned the handle and opened the heavy door, not needing to use the tumbler to unlock the safe. He only fully locked it when he left the office. He placed the envelope inside.

She waited until he was back behind the desk, facing her. "Where are we going out for drinks tonight?"

He shrugged. "I hadn't thought about it. Maybe Henney's."

She frowned. "I don't want to go to just another bar. I want to go someplace nice where I don't look out of place for wearing a skirt."

"Okay, I'll try to figure a place. There could be repercussions if we're seen together."

"I don't want to be sneaking around. You said you'd tell her you wanted a divorce. When is that going to happen?"

"It's complicated. I need to figure out how not to give her half of my business."

"You're a smart guy with a lawyer on call. Get it done." She gave him a smile. "I'm going home to change. I have a sexy new dress I know you'll like. Later." She waved goodbye.

He waited until he heard her close the main office door. "Fuck, this is getting out of hand." He used his mobile to call a frequent number and turned his chair to face away from the desk. "Hey, it's me. I want to see you soon." He waited for the reply. "Good. Tomorrow, at our usual place at seven. I have a new toy for you." His next call went to a restaurant where he made reservations. Next, he left a voice message for his wife, explaining he would be working late. He momentarily wondered why she didn't answer her phone. "She's likely with Paige. They sure spend a lot of time together." He worked on documents, finally shutting down his computer after inputting data into two spreadsheets.

Ryan stood and went to the closet in his office, pulling out a tie. As he fixed the knot, his thoughts went to what kind of dress Melisa was going to wear. He locked the safe, shut off the lights to the office, closed the door and took the elevator to the underground carpark. The drive to Melisa's apartment didn't take long. He went up to her apartment, where she let him in wearing a satin robe.

"I'll be just a minute." She handed him a glass of wine and disappeared into one of the two bedrooms.

Ryan watched her leave in the short, blue patterned robe, and continued to look at the open bedroom door from where she disappeared. Eventually, he peered around the living room, his attention drawn to the long, narrow photograph of Amsterdam on one wall. On the opposite wall was a photo of the Dubai. He remembered her telling him those were her two favourite cities she had been to.

Melisa stepped back into the living room, her high heels announcing her arrival. The green min-dress had a sheen to it. The front had a scooped neck, and as she pivoted in a circle, showed off a bare back. "You like?"

"You look gorgeous. Very sexy."

"I told you we should go to places other than a bar. I can't wear a dress like this just anywhere."

He nodded, feeling uncomfortable with her wanting a closer relationship. The lie he told her about wanting a divorce was causing issues. He exchanged kisses with her in the elevator and held her hand as he escorted her to his car. She stood by the passenger door, waiting for him to open it and close it after she was seated. He walked around the vehicle, a red Camero, and started the motor. He listened to the rumble of the motor and glanced at her legs. The dress had risen, showing off the distracting legs. He took a deep breath.

He drove slower that normal, occasionally placing a hand on her thigh. She didn't react, as if she was expecting the additional attention. He parked the car, opening the passenger door and helping her up. She walked confidently with him to the restaurant.

After they passed the front desk, Ryan noticed heads turned toward her as they made their way between tables. The maître d took care in helping her sit.

Ryan sat with his back to the wall, across from the small table from

Melisa. He noticed she looked very pleased with the attention she was receiving. The waiter was equally attentive, quickly bringing water and the menus. Ryan hoped all the attention remained on her and not on himself. He looked around the dining room and was relieved he didn't recognize anyone. He took a drink of his water, looking past her.

"Hey, look at me." She waited until he looked back at her. "Let's enjoy our meal together. No one knows you're here."

"Alright. I just have to be careful, that's all."

"If you're worried about being caught, the answer is simple. Tell her you want a divorce. You want one, and she probably just wants a cheque to say goodbye."

"We've been through this. I can't afford a messy breakup. The divorce will have to wait until I can hide the extra income. Right now, it'd cost me too much."

"Then the solution is simple. Have her knocked off." She gave a smile. "Just kidding."

Ryan studied her face, not seeing any sign she wasn't serious. *She's a dangerous woman.*

7

Thursday Afternoon

ROVER DRISCOLL PARKED HIS TRUCK IN FRONT OF THE BUNGALOW, WHERE A crew of three men were working on the roof. A fourth man was on the driveway, loading bundles of asphalt tiles on a conveyer belt that carried them to the roof. He walked over to the man loading the tiles.

"How's it going, Jimmy?" He knew Jimmy had served time for assault that resulted in surgery for the victim. He had empathy for his situation.

After they released Jimmy from prison, he felt tempted to return to return to the old way of life when the church contacted him, offering him an opportunity to live a normal life.

The man took a deep breath. "Damn hard work. But I ain't complaining. I sure appreciate you giving me a job."

Rover looked at the ex-con, recognizing the relief of actually working for a living. It reminded him of himself, several years ago, when the church sponsored him with an apartment and a modest income until he found a job. That helping hand allowed him to turn his back on his previous life. He returned the favour by hiring ex-cons who showed a willingness to start a new life. "I know how it is, Jimmy. Been there myself."

"Thanks. I'm willing to do all the overtime you want, even at straight time. I can use a few extra bucks." He loaded a bundle of tiles. "My ex never asked for child support payments. I guess she figured that was a dead end since I was in prison. But I want to send her some money. You know, to show her I'm not a complete asshole. If there's anything extra I can do, let me know."

"Well, actually there is a job outside of roofing I need a man for. It is illegal, but the Lord would tell you it's the right thing to do."

"As long as I don't get in trouble with the law."

"Trust me, the law won't care about this."

8

Friday Night, August 10

RACHEL SIPPED AT HER GLASS OF WINE, WAITING. THE HOTEL ROOM WAS well appointed, with a separate room containing the bed. She had mixed feelings of anticipation and guilt. Then a rise of anger as she thought about how she ended up where she was. She took another drink of her wine and refilled the glass.

A knock on the door set her in motion. She set her glass on the coffee table, checking her appearance in the mirror mounted on the wall. Rachel closed her terry-towel robe and peered through the eyepiece in the door, confirming his identity. She opened the door.

"Hi there," she breathed out.

"Hello, yourself." Ryan stepped inside and pushed the door closed. He tossed a leather duffle bag on the floor and grabbed her hair, pulling her head back.

She tried to meet his gaze. Suddenly, his mouth was on hers and she closed her eyes, dropping her arms to her sides. When he released her, she gasped and grabbed at his arm.

"Pour me a drink." He scanned the room, noting the hide-a-bed, two armchairs, the coffee table, and a desk.

She hurried to the table. "It's a really nice red."

Ryan walked over to the window, staring briefly between the parted drapes. He turned around and took the offered glass from Rachel. He studied the wine as he swirled the liquid around. "Tell me, are you expected home tonight?"

"Yes, but I told Joe I was going shopping with a girlfriend and then we'd go for drinks. I can stay out fairly late."

"Good." He tasted the wine and nodded his approval as set his glass on the desk. He used one hand to hold the lapel of her robe, and with the other hand, he slapped her face.

"Please. I don't want any marks on my face. I don't want to explain that to him."

He cupped his hand under her chin. "I'll decide what I do with you. Do you understand?"

"Yes. I just don't want to get caught."

He yanked opened her robe, pulling the material down her arms to the elbows. "That's not my problem. I'll do what I want with you." His hand squeezed her bare breast.

Rachel gasped. "Ryan..."

He pushed her toward the couch until she fell backward on the cushions. His eyes narrowed as he leered at her, the robe open in the middle, exposing her body. Ryan unbuckled his belt and pulled it loose. "Now it's time to have some fun. Roll over."

Rachel opened her mouth, unable to speak as she gulped in air, and twisted around to lie on her stomach.

———

RYAN CHECKED HIS MESSAGES AND PLACED HIS MOBILE ON THE TABLE AT the side of the queen-sized bed. "I think I'll order up some food. Afterward, there're some more things I want to do with you." He bent over her and untied the rope securing her wrists behind her back, observing the red stripes on her bottom.

Rachel turned around and sat on the bed. "Ryan, please, you know I'll do what you want. Delete those pictures. What if someone discovers them?"

"No, I enjoy looking at them. Don't worry, they're our secret. It also ensures your compliance with my wants."

Rachel stood at the side of the bed, rubbing her wrists. "Please."

"I'm keeping the photos. The subject is closed."

Rachel stared at his back as he left the bedroom. She let out a long breath and pushed away the rope to the end of the bed where the ball gag, more rope, and a riding crop rested. She stood, put on the housecoat, and walked to where he stood talking on the hotel room phone.

"Could you order me a salad and a burger as well? I'm hungry."

"You should eat, because I plan to test your endurance."

9

Saturday Morning

JOSEPH LOOKED UP FROM HIS NEWSPAPER HE WAS READING. NEXT TO HIS easy chair in the living room sat a table with a cup of coffee on a coaster. He saw Rachel come down from the staircase where the bedrooms were located and past the dining room to the kitchen. He waited until she reappeared, carrying a cup of coffee.

"I didn't hear you come home last night."

"The girls and I were having too much fun, and we ended up going for a late-night snack. I tried to be quiet, so I wouldn't disturb you." Rachel was glad they each had their own bedroom, and he wouldn't have seen the marks on her body.

"Who were the other girls?"

"I don't think you know them. One was my hairdresser, Teresia, and her sister, Alison, and also Marcia."

"I wish you had called or text me you would be staying out late. I was worried that you may be in trouble. I tried texting you, but you didn't respond."

"I'm sorry. I had my phone in my purse and didn't hear it." Rachel walked to a loveseat and carefully sat.

"Are you alright?"

"Yes, my back is sore. I must have slept wrong last night." She took a drink of her coffee. "I hope you don't mind my going out with the girls. Teresia is going through a bit of a rough patch and needs some cheering up."

"Where did you end up going?"

"A couple of places. We finished at The Cabin downtown."

He folded the newspaper back to its original configuration. "Where are your car keys? It needs an oil change and likely could use a car wash as well."

"Oh, thank you. I can never remember when it needs an oil change. The keys are in my purse."

Joseph walked to the dining room where her purse sat on the table. He opened the large purse, frowning at how full it was. He found the keys by a small bottle of skin lotion with the name Marriott Hotel stamped across it.

"I'll be back by lunchtime." He approached her, bending to give her a kiss, and exited to a side door that led to the garage.

The red Camry rolled down the street. Joseph was pleased he had convinced Rachel to buy the Toyota rather than a sportier Audi she had wanted, stressing the reliability of the Camry made it a better value. He suspected the reason she didn't look after her car as well as she should was because it wasn't her first choice.

He reached the quick lube service centre and didn't have a long wait before they began work changing the oil. He declined extra service options, insisting an oil change and filter was all the car required. Joseph cleaned out the inside of the vehicle, throwing away a tissue, candy wrappers, and an empty tube of lipstick. He found several receipts, including three from valet parking at the Marriott Hotel.

He stared at the receipts. The last one was dated from last night and time stamped from early evening to midnight. The other parking receipts had similar time references on different dates.

After the oil change, he took the vehicle to a car wash. As he stood behind the glass partition, watching the workers wash the cars, he pulled out the parking receipts from his shirt pocket, wondering if his suspicions were true.

10

Monday Evening

THE PHONE CALL FROM JOSEPH, WHO NORMALLY DIDN'T ASK HIM TO JOIN him for social drinks surprised Michael. He parked his car and stepped inside the Homefire Grill restaurant. Just past the entrance, a woman stood behind a pedestal. She gave him a welcoming smile.

"Do you have a reservation for this evening?"

"No, I'm actually meeting a friend in the lounge." He turned to his right and entered the lounge, spotting Joseph at the booth along the back wall. As he crossed the floor, he saw Joseph was drinking a dark beer, not looking happy.

"Hi, Joseph. Good to see you again."

Joseph nodded. "Thanks for coming out."

Michael sat. "No problem." He studied the drink menu when a server arrived at the table. He pointed at Joseph's beer. "I'll have what he's having." He turned his attention to Joseph. "What's going on? You look worried."

Joseph shook his head. "I don't know what to do, and I'm scared of what may happen. I'm between two bad alternatives."

"What is it, Joseph? Your health?"

"No, not that." He took a drink of his beer. "I need to talk to someone, but you've got to promise to keep this to yourself."

"I can do that."

Joseph waited until the server dropped off Michael's beer. "Last night Rachel went out. A girls' night out. She said they went to a couple of places and ended up in a bar downtown. She went out by herself last week as well, to this bar that had salsa dancing. I don't like to dance, so I didn't mind when she said was going there with a girlfriend."

"Okay, so she's going out without you with some friends. I suspect that isn't uncommon with wives."

"I know. But I found parking receipts in her car. They were all dated for when she went out, and all of them were for a hotel." He took another drink with a shaking hand. "I think Rachel is having an affair." He looked down at the table.

"Jesus." Michael paused, thinking about how to respond. "She just left her car there and travelled in another car. You know, to save time and gas."

"Maybe, but I doubt it. The parking receipt was at the same Mariott Hotel as the other receipts."

"Who were the other girls she went out with? Can you verify she went out with them?"

"She said they weren't people I knew."

"Gee, man, I don't know what to tell you. Look, there could be a reasonable explanation for the parking at the hotel. Maybe she paid it for a friend. I think you should sit down with her and ask her."

"I thought about that." His face turned red. "But if it's true she's having an affair, then what? Maybe she'll ask for a divorce." His eyes became wet. "I don't want to lose her."

Michael turned around and signalled for the server to bring another round of drinks. "Look, you have to find out one way or another, don't you? Maybe if she had an affair, you could go for counselling and patch things up."

Joseph sighed. "I'm not a very good husband. I'm too picky about any little mess. We sleep in separate bedrooms because I have sleep apnea. I'm out of shape and it's been weeks since we've had sex." He waited as the server placed the two pints on the table. "I can't blame her if she wants someone else. If I confront her on this parking, I'm worried she'll walk out of my life."

Michael stared at his beer, turning glass in his hands before taking a drink. "Okay, let's go over a few things we know. One, she married you, knowing who you are. That means love. Two, she hasn't asked for a divorce. You can still keep her. You just need a strategy."

"What do you suggest?"

"What does she like? Try cooking her favourite meal. You said she likes to dance. Take her dancing."

"I don't how to cook or dance."

"Cooking is easy. Just look on the internet for a recipe. Even if doesn't turn out, she'll appreciate the effort. Just open a good bottle of wine and the dinner will be a success. As far as dancing, take her out on the floor and shuffle your feet. Everyone will watch her, not you."

Joseph nodded. "You're right. No matter what happens, I better at least try. Thanks, buddy. I didn't know who to talk to at first, but it occurred to me of all the guys I know, you always had a good head for problem solving."

Michael picked up his glass and tapped it against Joseph's. "To your success."

"Thanks. I'm not sure if I'm glad I found those receipts. Perhaps ignorance is best."

"No, knowledge gives you an opportunity to make things better. By the way, which Mariott was it?"

"The one downtown, just off Jasper Avenue."

———

MICHAEL DROVE BACK TO HIS CONDO. WHEN HE STOPPED AT A SET OF lights, his fingers drummed on the steering wheel. He didn't believe it was a coincidence that Rachel's parking receipts were from the same hotel as the one he found in Ryan's car.

Michael considered he had once been a close friend of Ryan. Then one summer, that had all changed. He wanted at the time to beat up the man who stole his girlfriend, or at the very least, having nothing to do with him again. But that would mean never seeing Brooke. Reluctantly, he maintained a relationship with Ryan, acting as if he had gotten past the betrayal. One thing he was always aware of was Ryan's lack of scruples. His favourite saying was, 'if you don't get caught, it ain't cheating'. He verbally told his mobile to call Ryan.

The phone rang and Ryan answered. "Hey, Michael, what's up?"

"I'm wondering if you're free tomorrow for a drink. There's a situation I want to talk to you."

"Sure. Anything important?"

"Just a problem I've come across. How about the Beer Revolution in Unity Square at seven?"

"Sounds good. See you then."

———

PAIGE BUTLER PARKED HER JEEP AND ENTERED THE DOUBLE TREE HOTEL. She briefly smoothed down the fabric of her dress and proceeded past the hotel lobby to the restaurant. She saw Ryan Morgan give her a wave where he sat opposite a woman with chestnut coloured hair. As she approached the table, she saw the woman appeared to be in her late thirties, medium build, but had a pleasant smile on her face.

Ryan stood. "Paige, this is Carol Madison, the CEO of Griffin Developments."

Paige shook her hand and sat, unsure of what to say if the conversation turned toward commercial real estate. Fortunately, the talk centred on vacations and travel. She mentioned her own preference for the Caribbean, and Carol responded with her agreement with her choice.

"There're few things better than relaxing on the beach, with no pressure other than ordering another margarita. Europe is wonderful, but there is so much to see and do that a holiday there can tire one out."

Paige noticed Ryan was content to let her talk with Carol. He ordered another bottle of wine to go with their dinner, but Paige was careful to restrain her drinking.

"I notice you're not wearing a ring. Haven't you found the right guy yet?"

Paige took her time by taking a sip of her wine. "Well, I recently broke up with someone. She was nice, but a little immature for my liking."

"Compatibility is important. I agree your interest in people should have a broader view of life. I believe we have common interests."

Paige nodded, carefully giving replies to Carol's inquires.

During dessert, Ryan finally spoke. "Carol, I don't want to rush you, but have you come to a decision on my proposal? I understand that your flight leaves in the morning, and I'd prefer if we can come to an agreement in person now, rather than long-distance communications later."

"Of course, I understand business needs. I wanted to meet you in person, to get a sense of who you are." She looked at Paige. "Your associate is very nice and I feel comfortable working with both of you. I will send you an electronic confirmation of our agreement when I return home."

Shortly after dessert, Ryan excused himself. "I have an early morning meeting, but I'll leave you ladies to continue your conversation." Paige watched as he paid for the bill, telling the server to add any additional expenses on to his card.

Paige was concerned when Carol suggested they resume their talk in the lounge, hoping she didn't get into an awkward situation. She sat, sipping on a diet cola drink.

"I'm under the impression you're not wanting to proceed a relationship with me. That's alright. I enjoyed our conversation. I have to catch a flight tomorrow morning, so I'll bid you goodnight. Perhaps our paths will cross again."

Paige gratefully said goodbye to Carol, giving her a hug before she left the lounge. She checked her cellphone, seeing message from Ryan.

'How did it go?'

She texted a reply. 'Next time you try this stunt, I'll kill you.'

11

Tuesday, August 14

RYAN YAWNED AS HE WAITED FOR THE COFFEEMAKER TO FILL A CUP FROM the capsule he had inserted moments before. He leaned on the granite counter.

"What time did you go to bed last night?" Brooke peered at him from the kitchen doorway.

"I don't know. After midnight."

"I know that. I went to bed at one. You still weren't home. Should I ask you what her name is?" She crossed her arms.

"There isn't anyone. I stay up late to unwind. Business pressure."

"You can stay up late here and drink as well."

"Cripes, so you can nag at me? I'm working hard to make money and I don't like being accused of stuff by you."

"We don't need more money. That's the one thing we have lots of."

"What do you want?" He walked past her to the dining room, where he sat at the head of the table.

"Ryan." She let out a sigh and followed him to the dining room. She sat at the corner next to him. She reached for his hand. "I want to try again for another. I'm ready."

Ryan stared at her. "I don't know. A kid would really mess up our plans to travel to Europe."

"We don't need to travel. We don't need another new car. What I want is to have a baby. If you don't want to have a family, then maybe we don't have a future together."

"You want a divorce because I don't want to have a baby in our lives right now?" He pulled his hand away.

"Ryan, I don't want a divorce. I want to have a baby with you. If you don't want a family, then you better be prepared for an expensive divorce. I know you're hiding money somewhere. New golf clubs. New motorbike. None of it paid for from our bank account or credit cards. Time is running out for you to decide."

Ryan took a drink of his coffee. "Look, I'm not saying no, just that you kind of dropped this on me." He stood. "I need another cup." He went to the kitchen and to the coffee machine. As the machine gurgled coffee into the cup, he looked at the kitchen knives in the rack on the counter. "Okay, you made your point. I'll give it some thought."

———

MICHAEL FINISHED HIS MORNING BUSINESS APPOINTMENT SHORTLY BEFORE eleven. The south side of Edmonton wasn't his usual area to meet with clients, and he pondered whether to have lunch in the area or go back to the downtown area where he had an office. The sight of a health food store triggered a memory, and he called Paige Butler, who worked at Women's Whole Body Gym.

"What's up, Michael?"

"I'm on the south side. Do you have time for lunch?"

"Sure. Where?"

"How about Hudson's? I can pick you up."

"No, it's close by. I'll walk over. See you in thirty minutes."

Michael drove a few blocks, finding a spot along the street. He paid for two hours and found a table at Hudson's outside on the patio. He ordered a beer and waited for Paige. A few minutes she arrived, wearing black yoga pants with coloured bands along the side and a bright yellow crop-top.

He grinned as she sat. "I suspect you gathered a few looks with your outfit."

"It's what I was wearing at the gym." She shrugged. "I'm going to wear stuff like this while I still can."

"Good for you. I'm betting there're a few men who will be disappointed if they learn you're playing for the other team."

She laughed. "Well, it's still good to be noticed. What's new with you?"

He waited as the waitress took their order and resumed speaking. "Just a few business deals, nothing special. But I'm curious if you know if there's anything is going on with Rachel."

"In what way?" Paige pursed her lips.

"Joseph is worried about her. You and Brooke hang around with her. What do you know?"

She took a drink of her water. "Rachel likes adventure. In more than one way." Paige bit her lower lip. "I don't want to say too much. Is there something specific?"

"Is she having an affair?"

Paige shook her head. "Not that I'm aware of, but she may be tempted. Rachel has complained about being bored in her marriage. She loves Joseph but, well, I'm speculating here, wants him to do more in the bedroom." She pointed a finger at him. "Now speak. What do you know?"

"Keep this to yourself. Tell no one. Joseph is worried Rachel is cheating on him. He found several parking stubs from the same hotel on different nights, nights she claimed she was somewhere else."

"Damn. No, I don't know anything more. Let's hope that Rachel was only having a fling. I don't want Joseph to get hurt. He's a good man." She smiled. "A little dull, but sincere."

"And a terrible golfer." He paused as the waitress dropped off their food order. "Let's keep this to ourselves. There's no point in spreading rumours."

"Fair enough." She took a bite of her food. "Back at the barbeque, you hinted at Ryan doing some business dealings that weren't kosher. What was that all about?"

Michael frowned before answering. "I don't get Ryan. He wasn't always like this, but as he gets older, he seemed less concerned about ethics. From what I heard, he's skimming cash from a bar he owns, or at least has a controlling interest in. He's also letting drugs be bought and sold inside. It's either causing, or is going to cause, a major problem with Rover. He invested with Ryan in this bar and is wondering why he's not getting a return on the investment. Ryan gave him a story that they had to repair stuff like the cooler, but that was bullshit."

"How do you know this?"

"I talked to a former manager of the bar now working at Earl's. He left when he saw what was going on. He didn't want any part of illegal books and the drug trade."

They finished their meal with small talk, watching people walk by the patio.

"How is your gym job going? You've been there for over a year." He ginned. "A new record for you."

Paige laughed. "It's good. I teach, I train, and I get to take some courses as well. All women too."

"I have this image of a bunch of ladies in yoga pants doing some stretching exercises. I can see why you enjoy working there."

"Men have a one-track mind." She shook her head and laughed.

"I plead guilty." He took a bite of his sandwich. "So what courses are you teaching at the gym?"

"Kick boxing and Muay Thai."

"Muay Thai?"

"Something like kick boxing, but with additional hits allowed. Excellent for self-defence." She paused. "And attacking."

"I guess I better not make you mad at me." He finished his beer. "Anything else you're up to besides getting paid to exercise?"

"Exercise? That's a damn weak description for a workout." She smiled at his tease. "Well, as a matter of fact, I'm getting paid to be an escort." She watched his eyes for his reaction.

"An escort?" He raised his eyebrows. "Tell me the story behind that."

"Okay. This is strictly confidential." She licked her lips. "Do you remember back in university I did modeling on the side?"

"Yeah, pictures you refused to show to the rest of us."

"Right, and for good reason." She looked down at the table and back at his eyes. "You know they were nudes, right?"

"I do. That's why I wanted to see them." He grinned at her. "You're a nice-looking woman both then and now."

"Thanks, but someone found the photographer who took the pictures. And he propositioned me."

"Really? Who was that?"

"Ryan." She stabbed a fork at the remains of her salad. "He showed me the photos on his computer and threatened to show them to others unless I agreed to help him secure a big contract by being nice to a female executive." She rolled her eyes. "That was last week."

"What the fuck? What did you tell him?"

"He also gave me five hundred bucks. I swore at him and told him this was a one and only time I'd act like an escort. The thing is, I don't really care about those photos. I was young and foolish. I just didn't like he was trying to blackmail me. The five hundred dollars would have done the same thing."

"Ryan can be a jerk. So, you don't care if others see the photos?"

"Not really. I'm proud of my body. I've had more photos done. You know, boudoir style."

"Will you show them to me?"

She paused and smiled. "Sure, providing you show me nude photos of you first."

He laughed. "I don't have the right body for that. But I'm willing to trade."

"I bet you are." She grinned and shook her head. "Next time you're at my place, I'll show some of them to you."

"Okay, I'll even remind you."

"I'm sure you will. Anyway, I was pissed at Ryan because he tried to blackmail me. If he had just offered the money and asked me to have dinner with this woman, I would have done so. Even without the money, I'd likely do it. But using those photos as leverage made me want to kill him. What a jerk."

"Ryan has trouble knowing right from wrong at times. It's always if it benefits himself."

"One of these times he's going to cross that line, and someone will take a strong exception to it."

"I agree. I do my best to be civil with him because he's married to Brooke. Otherwise, I'd have nothing to do with him."

"I remember at one time he was your best friend. That was before that summer."

"Yes. My fault. I went to Prince George to work that summer and broke our triangle."

"How were you to know that Ryan was going to do what he did? He worked on her all summer while you're away. Ryan got her drunk, they smoked up and she ended up pregnant. He was jealous of our triangle and broke it, not you."

"I should've given her a ring before I left."

"Hindsight. You showed up at the wedding, which surprised me."

"What surprised me was that I didn't punch him out."

"I know." She reached over and touched his hand. "You're a good man. Besides Brooke, you're my best friend."

"Thanks."

"And maybe Brooke and Ryan won't be together forever. Just saying."

————

MICHAEL ARRIVED AT BEER REVOLUTION EARLY, DECIDING TO EAT AT THE popular restaurant. The large overhead TV screens showed a listing of the current beers on tap. He picked an IPA and ordered a pizza. He was on his second beer when Ryan walked into the bar. Michael signalled him over at his table.

After the server took his order, Ryan asked why he wanted to speak with him. "It sounded important. Are you in difficulties?"

"No, I'm doing good. Business is picking up. How's things on your end? Anything new?"

"Ah, just the bar is using up a lot of my time. When I bought the place, I didn't realize how much time I'd have to invest in it. Maintenance, liquor orders and fighting with the brewery. Customers get real upset when their favourite brew runs dry. My manager quit on me with just a week's notice, and I had to scramble to find a replacement. So, why did you call this meeting?"

"Just a few rumours I heard." Michael picked up a chicken wing from the platter. "Are you having marriage problems, Ryan? Someone said they saw you with another woman at a hotel."

Ryan paused from taking a drink of his ale. "What? No, it wasn't me."

"Okay, I just wanted to ask as a friend."

"No, not me. Which hotel was it?"

"The Marriott downtown."

"No, I never go there, so it wasn't me."

"That's good to hear." Michael reached for another chicken wing. He looked at Ryan, who didn't show any sign he was lying. "Say, have you talked to Paige lately? I was trying to reach her and could only leave a message on her phone."

Ryan shook his head. "No, last time I saw her was at the barbeque." Ryan swung around and drew the waitress's attention. "Bring me another beer and another order of hot wings." He gave a smirk as he watched the server walk away. "Too bad Paige is a lesbian. She sure is a good-looking woman."

"Yeah, she is. Paige is also smart and knows martial arts. She's a great friend, but I sure wouldn't want to piss her off. She's an expert in martial arts. I suspect she could kick our asses without breaking into a sweat." For the first time, Ryan showed a reaction, pausing before he took a drink, his eyes looking like his hand was caught in a cookie jar.

Michael insisted on paying for the bill. "I called you, so my treat. You can buy me a beer at our next golf game."

———

THE TRAFFIC LIGHT TURNED GREEN, AND MICHAEL SQUEEZED THE steering wheel, as he thought out loud. "You selfish, lying bastard. Screwing up the marriage of Rachel and Joseph. Brooke deserves better. Much better. And blackmailing Paige! Enough is enough." A horn sounded behind him and he stepped on the gas. "There's one way to handle this. One definite solution."

12

August 18, Saturday Morning

JOSEPH CLOSED HIS BEDROOM DOOR, GLANCING AT HIS WIFE'S DOOR AS HE made his way to the stairs. He was asleep when she came home last night, and he suspected there wasn't any need to make extra coffee for her. Her usual routine on weekends was to stay up late and sleep in. Weekdays were different, but she rarely had time for a coffee before heading off to work.

He didn't mind the quiet mornings. He would make himself a coffee, listen to music, and read. This morning he didn't feel like reading and took his coffee mug downstairs to his workshop. The simple workbench held a modest collection of tools and a set of knives. The six knives were resting in a wooden case with an empty spot for a seventh knife. Joseph had bought the knife set second hand with the missing knife. He purchased a replacement knife, a long-bladed style. It didn't fit in the case and rested next to a wood figure he was working on. The horse was taking shape, and to his credit, looked like it was meant to be a horse all along, and not the unicorn he had first envisioned.

He picked up a knife and whittled the wood closer to the horse shape. Later, he heard footsteps upstairs. He carefully put down the knife and went upstairs with his empty mug.

"Good morning," he called out. "I'll make a pot of coffee."

"Thanks. I need a cup."

Joseph frowned when he saw her; the messy hair, the lack of makeup and the terry-towel housecoat did not show her in the best light. He adjusted his voice to sound cheerful. "Did you have a good time last night with your friends?" He pressed a button on the machine, and it began gurgling, sending drips of black coffee into the pot.

"Yes, it was good."

Together, they stared at the pot. He wasn't sure what to say, and she appeared too tired to speak.

"Where did you end up going?"

The coffee machine finished its task. She poured herself a coffee and faced him. "Different places. I had a bit too much to drink, so I stayed longer until I felt safe to drive."

He nodded as he wondered why she spent more effort getting dressed up for a night with her friends than when on the rare occasion they went out together. This morning she looked tired and older than her years. He knew he was not without his faults in appearance, putting on too much weight on his waistline. At one time he was slim and athletic, enjoying competitive swimming at university. Over the years, he accepted this was where he was in life. The strong, confident man that married the cheerleader became only a memory.

"I have some errands to run. You stay home and relax."

"Thanks. I think I'll sit outside with my coffee." She gave him a forced smile.

"I'll make dinner tonight."

"Really? That will be nice. You don't normally cook."

"Not normal times. I want to do more things around here."

RACHAEL ENJOYED THE COFFEE AS SHE SAT IN THE BACKYARD PATIO. THE morning sun felt good as she held the cup. Her smile turned to a frown as her mind wandered to last night. She wondered why she allowed herself to become trapped into an affair with Ryan. Dread of what she was becoming replaced the excitement of their first rendezvous and his use of cuffs on her. She took another drink of her coffee, finding it had turned bitter.

She returned inside, refilling the cup, but this time with more milk. Rachael sat in the living room. Joseph's easy chair looked inviting, and she eased herself onto the soft cushion. The coffee tasted better this time, and she looked for a spot on the side table to set it down. A book on the table lay face down, and she picked it up. It was titled Weight Loss For Men, and she open the book where he had dog-eared a page. The section stressed exercise was an important component for weight control.

Rachael closed the book, replacing it where she found it. She saw earlier in the week a payment to a gym and had meant to ask him about it. Now it seemed to her it was part of his decision to get healthier. She finished her coffee and went upstairs, wanting to attempt to look better when he returned home.

13

Saturday Evening

RACHEL RELAXED IN THE LIVING ROOM, DRINKING A GLASS OF WHITE WINE her husband had poured from the chilled bottle. She called out, "What's the occasion?" Earlier, she decided if her husband was going to cook dinner, she should dress up a bit. She spent more time in front of the mirror, trying to hide a small bruise on her left jaw.

Joseph stepped out of the kitchen, looking nervous. "There isn't one. I decided I wanted to do something special for you." He gave her an anxious smile. "Providing I don't burn dinner."

She watched him disappear into the kitchen and wondered about the change in him over the past few days. First, was the discovery of a diet book he had bought, and then the purchase of a gym membership he had purchased. He was still neat in his appearance but had stopped reading the daily newspaper for an hour in the evening, putting it away after a few minutes and initiating a conversation with her.

Rachel didn't know why the sudden change but was she thankful for it. It made her feel guilty about her affair with Ryan.

"Dinner is about to be served." Joseph carried out two plates and set them down on the dining room table.

Rachel stood and walked over. "It looks wonderful and smells delicious. Where did you learn to cook?"

He grinned. "Google." He refilled her wineglass. He sat and continued the conversation. "The truth is, I feel I've been neglecting you, or at least not doing more to let you know how much I love you. This dinner is one way to show you how important you are to me."

Rachel took in a deep breath. "I love you, too. This is wonderful, the dinner, you, I, and a chance to talk."

She enjoyed the meal. The salmon was a bit dry, and the salad wasn't properly tossed, but to her it was the best meal she had in a long time. They opened a second bottle of wine, and rather than watch TV, as was their norm, listened to music in the living room.

Rachel gave Joseph a kiss as they sat on the couch. "I'll be back in a minute." She went upstairs to her bedroom, undressed, and put on her dressing gown. It was black, lacy, and something she hadn't worn for years. She checked her hair and makeup and ventured downstairs. She took her time reaching for her wineglass and taking a drink, pleased at his reaction as she stood in front of him. Rachel placed her empty glass on a table and reached for his hand. "Come with me."

Joseph swallowed and followed her to her bedroom.

Later that night, she listened to his heavy breathing, turned toward him, and cried.

———

IN THE MORNING, RACHEL INFORMED JOSEPH SHE WOULD MAKE BREAKFAST, and cooked bacon and eggs. It mildly surprised her he turned down the offer of toast, telling her he was cutting down on certain foods.

"It is either lose a few pounds or buy new clothes. The diet is cheaper." He chuckled.

"I think you look fine the way you are."

"Thank you." He gave her a kiss. "Now, I'm going to make use of my gym membership. I'll be back in a couple of hours. Perhaps we can take in a movie tonight. I know you like horror flicks, so let's see that one that they're advertising on TV."

"That would be great." She watched him leave via the door to the garage, and immediately called a familiar number, reaching a voice mail.

"Hi, it's me. Look, I don't know how to say this, so I'll come right out with it. I don't want to see you anymore. Joseph and I are working things out, and we can't continue with our rendezvous anymore. Goodbye."

Rachel closed her eyes, hoping that would be the end of their affair. The problem, she knew, was Ryan didn't take rejection well. Her hope changed to thoughts of desperation.

14

Monday Evening

Ryan finished his drink at the Hi-Lite Bar and signaled the waitress to come over to his table.

"Another scotch?"

"Yes, but where is Mitch? You said he had stepped out for more supplies and wouldn't be long."

"He should be back soon." She picked up the empty glass and shifted her hips. She noticed that, unlike the regulars, he was dressed up in a suit jacket. That meant there was a chance of a better tip. She also knew he was the owner of the bar, and it wouldn't hurt to be on his good side. "I'll get you another scotch. By the way, my name is Jill." She walked away with a stride that was accented by her tight blue jeans.

Shortly later, Mitch arrived in the bar. The waitress pointed at Ryan, and he made his way over.

"Hi, Ryan. What brings you here?" The tall, slim man sat across from Ryan.

"A couple of things. One is our business relationship. From now on I want you to make the cash delivery. I don't want a bunch of unknowns coming to me with an envelope full of bills. That's not smart or secure."

"I was busy. I have the bar to run."

"Figure it out. You make those deliveries personally. Clear?"

"Alright, alright."

"What's the other thing?"

"You can cover my tab, then send that waitress back over here."

A few minutes later, the waitress came back to his table. "Is everything okay?"

"Yup, just fine." He put a twenty-dollar bill on the table. "Your tip. Tell me, do you model on the side? You have a pretty face and I'd like to have a few photos done of you."

"Sometimes." She gave him a smile.

He took her name and phone number, telling her he would call her soon. After she left, he listened to his voice messages, cursing as he listened to Rachel's voice. "No way you're walking away from me just like that." He wanted to call her back right away but didn't think she would answer a call from him if Joseph was nearby. Instead, he called Melisa.

"Hey, how about I pick you up in an hour?" He listened to her reply. "Sure, I'll take you to a nice place." He broke off the connection. "Damn, she's getting to be high maintenance. And this bit about me getting a divorce so I can be with her? She ain't that good in bed."

15

Tuesday

"RACHEL, THERE'S SOMEONE TO SEE YOU." THE TALL BRUNETTE PEERED down at the desk cluttered with files. A monitor showed a screen full of unread emails. The brunette gave her a smile. "You need a break from this." She pointed at the front counter. "He said his name was Ryan Morgan."

Rachel stopped breathing and her heart pounded in her chest. She wanted to stay in her cubicle, wanted to ignore the front counter and work on the schedule.

"Are you alright?"

Rachel stood, her hand pushing at the desk. "I'm fine. Just a headache." She made her way to the counter and the grim face of Ryan. His smile looked forced at her approach. She stopped at the counter, took a deep a breath and tried to look at his eyes.

"We need to talk. Now."

Her gaze dropped to his chest. "Please go. Leave me alone."

"No, you're not in any position to walk away from me. We can talk right here, or we can go for a coffee. But we will have a conversation. Now."

Rachel turned to the watching faces at the desks near the counter. "I'll be back soon." She stepped around the counter, crossing her arms. When she reached the glass doors, she pushed one open and let it swing back at his approach. She jabbed at the elevator button.

"Don't think for a minute this attitude is going to help you." He hissed at her ear. "There'll be consequences."

The elevator doors opened, and she stepped inside, fighting back tears. "I know there'll be consequences. But maybe not just for me. Maybe you'll face some consequences too."

He pressed a hand against her chest, pushing her to the corner of the car. "Don't threaten me. I hold all the cards. Or in this case, the pictures." He released her when the doors opened, and they walked to the cafeteria, sitting at a table near the corner of the pedestrian looking interior.

"You seem to forget that I've control over you. So far, I've only called you when you're free of obligations to meet me. But that can change in a hurry."

"This isn't just about us. I owe it to Joseph to be faithful. I feel guilty about what I've done. Please, please, please. Forget about me and delete those pictures."

He shook his head. "Not happening. This Saturday, you will learn a few lessons on obedience. Understood?"

She meekly nodded. "I hear exactly what you're saying." She met his gaze, not flinching this time.

Rachel returned to her workstation. She was glad the padded cubicle walls gave her some privacy. This time her headache was real, and she took out two pills from a bottle in her desk drawer. The brunette approached her again. "Can I help?"

Rachel's hand shook as she tried to rest it on the keyboard. "No, but I'll be okay."

"You look awful. You shouldn't be at work." She rested a hand on her shoulder, causing her to jump.

A tear ran down as she tried to compose herself. Her lips parted, but words refused to form.

"Come with me. I'll sign you out sick for the rest of the day. Can you drive? I can call you a cab if you like."

"I, I can drive."

Rachel tried to keep her composure as she reached the elevator, frowning when she saw others in the car. When she reached the lower parking level, she rushed to her Camry, locking herself in the vehicle, sobbing.

An hour passed before she felt strong enough to drive home. The empty house was comforting to her, and she poured herself a straight rum, staring at the walls in the living room. A second drink soon followed.

———

SHE JUMPED WHEN SHE HEARD A DOOR OPEN AND CLOSE. JOSEPH ENTERED the room. He greeted her, "You beat me home." He noticed the frozen expression on her face and the drink in her hand. "Is something wrong?"

She nodded. "Please sit down. I have something awful to tell you."

He went to his easy chair, sitting stiffly, and watched as she put her drink on a corner table. Instead of sitting in another chair, she kneeled in front of him.

Tears rolled down her cheeks. "Please forgive me. I've been stupid, selfish, unfaithful and now have put us in an embarrassing situation." She took a deep, shuddering breath. "I had an affair. I'm so sorry." She looked up at him. His jaw was quivering, and his face was turning pale. "Please, can we work through this? I promise I'll never cheat on you again."

He stared at her with his breathing rapid. Rachel became alarmed he was going to have a heart attack. "Joseph?"

He finally nodded. "You want to stay with me?"

"Yes. I'll do anything. Please forgive me."

He leaned back his head and slowly exhaled. "Thank God." He

focused on her. "Of course, I forgive you. I don't want to lose you. Just tell me the affair is over."

"It is, but he has photos of me, and is threatening to show them. I don't know what to do."

"Who is he?"

Rachel looked at the floor. "Ryan."

"That son-of-a-bitch. That fucking son-of-a-bitch."

She looked up in surprise. She couldn't remember the last time she had heard him swear. "Please don't do anything. I just wanted you to be prepared if the photos show up."

"You were naked in them?"

"Worse. He also had me tied up."

His hands became fists. "I see. Does he want money for them?"

"No. He just wants me to continue to see him."

"Okay. I'll deal with him later. Right now, I think I'll join you in a drink."

She quickly got up. "I'll get you one. Scotch?"

"Please." He watched her hurry to the dining room, where they kept a small liquor cabinet. He wondered why she had an affair and with Ryan, of all people. He was curious if he forced her to be tied up, or if she liked it. *I need to do more to please her. I won't risk losing her again. As for Ryan, he is going to learn the hard way I'm no pushover when it comes to protecting my wife.*

16

August 22, Wednesday

ROVER FROWNED AS HE WAITED IN RYAN'S FRONT OFFICE. HE OBSERVED Melisa step past her desk and opened the door to Ryan's office. A moment later, she signaled for him to enter the second office.

"Hey, Rover, what brings you here? Have a seat."

Rover pulled a chair to the desk and grunted as he sat. He closed his hand and used a thumb to point at the door behind him. "What's with her? Can she actually type and file?"

"She does. What's it to you?"

"I've seen longer skirts on a cheerleader. Does Brooke know about her?"

"She knows enough. I have a receptionist. Was I supposed to not hire her just because she's good-looking?"

"I'm just wondering why you'd put yourself within temptation." He tapped a finger on the edge of the desk. "Your receptionist is not my concern. However, your earlier assurances I would receive payment from my investment with your property management firm have not born fruit. I will overlook that you used my investment to support the operation of a bar, as I used to frequent such places myself before I found the Lord. But my patience is wearing thin."

"There's been some unfortunate expenses. The refrigeration unit needed repair, there was a flood causing damages, including the electrical. I had to shut down the bar for a while during the repairs. I had to pay emergency hour prices to get stuff fixed."

"That may be true. But I see you spending money like there's no tomorrow. New golf clubs, weekend trip to Vegas, a car only six months old." He frowned. "It looks to me like you're making money on your investments, but I got diddly squat from the same investment. You know what I'm saying?"

"I hear you. But I have more than one channel of investments. I actually sunk my own money into the bar to keep it afloat. I promise you, you'll start getting a return on your money now that the bar is back to normal."

"Okay. But, as I said, my patience is running thin. You may not like it when it runs out. Understood?"

"I hear you. No worries." He gave a grin.

Rover stood, his face passive. "I'll be seeing you soon." He exited out of the office.

Ryan's grin disappeared. "Fuck."

———

ROVER DROVE HIS TRUCK, THINKING ABOUT HIS CONVERSATION WITH RYAN. It had left a sour taste in his mouth when he saw the grin on his face, like someone who had just pulled a fast one on an unsuspecting friend. *I ain't that naïve to think you're telling me the complete truth.* On an impulse, he changed directions of his truck, heading to an area of he hadn't frequented in the past few years. He parked his truck, memories of the bars along the block came back to him. Some the names had changed, but inside they were the same as they always were. He stepped into the Hi-Lite Bar and Grill.

His eyes adjusted to the darkened interior, and the smell of the bar was too familiar. *No drinking here. You made that promise with the Lord.* He sat at a high-top table near the bar, scanning around. The clicking of balls from the pool table made him feel slightly better. *I used to be pretty damn good at that game.*

"What can I get you? Just a drink or do you want to see a menu too?" The petite waitress gave him a smile.

"I'll take a ginger ale and a menu, please."

Rover looked at the bar. The shelves at the back were well-stocked, including a few premium brands.

"Here's the menu." She placed the laminated sheet on the table along with the soft drink.

"Thanks. Anything you recommend, or to avoid here? By the way, the name is Rover."

"Hi. Jill. Good to meet you. Avoid the fish. Everything else is pretty good."

"Good to know. How's business here?"

"Slow right now, but it gets full at night."

"I guess you'd prefer working nights. Better tips."

"Yeah, but everyone has to do a few afternoon shifts."

"You been working here long?"

"Almost two years."

"I'll take the chicken burger with fries."

"Okay, coming right up."

Rover studied the bar, not seeing anything unusual. By the time he had emptied his glass of pop, Jill had returned with his meal.

"Refill?"

"Please. Tell me, was this bar shut down for repairs last month? A heard a bar in this area had a lot of problems with flooding and the cooler stop working."

"Not here. This bar has been busy ever since I've been here, and it hasn't ever had any flooding or cooler problem. Maybe it was a bar down the street."

"Could be. Thanks."

Rover ate his meal, contemplating what he would like to do to Ryan.

17

Thursday Morning

MELISA REGAN WALKED DOWN THE BUILDING HALLWAY, STOPPING AT THE door of Ryan Morgan Commercial Reality. She dug out a set of keys from her purse, unlocked the door and stepped inside. The light switch was just past the doorway, and she flipped the switches on, revealing the modern office furnishings. The walls showed the brick interior, providing a contrast to the rest of the contemporary office.

Melisa went past the sitting area for guests and to a walk-in closet size area. The room had a small storage area, but also included a sink and a coffee machine. She turned on the machine, inserted a coffee capsule, and heard the humming sound as it brewed a cup of coffee. She wiped the area around the machine, tossing the paper towel in the garbage.

The coffee was ready, and she added cream to the black liquid, carrying the cup to her desk at the front of the office. Next to her desk, a doorway led to Ryan Morgan's private office. She sat at her desk, relaxing in the comfortable five-legged chair as she nursed her coffee. After the cup was empty, she walked around the visitors' area of the office, placing magazines back in order on a coffee table. It was at the table she spotted the three glasses, one with a gold liquid remaining. Melisa frowned and carried the glasses to the back. Underneath the coffee machine was a dishwasher, and she placed the glassware inside.

Curious why there were three glasses on the table, Melisa ventured into Ryan Morgan's office. On the desk, she spotted a bottle of Tennessee whisky. Annoyed that it appeared Morgan had guests in the office drinking whisky after she had left, she let out a long sigh. She checked the safe, finding it locked. Most mornings she checked the safe, hoping he had forgotten to lock it the night before. There was a lot of untraceable cash in the safe, she knew, and she was willing to take a small portion. Not enough that he would notice or would know for certain it had been stolen.

On top of the safe was a camera case. She unzipped the top, taking out the black-body camera, recognizing it from the one Ryan used to take her photos. Melisa turned the camera on, switching to the review mode. She studied the images on the LCD display, glaring at the semi-nude blonde pictures. Annoyed, she shut off the camera and returned it to its case.

She returned to her desk and checked her mobile for text messages and social media. She used unique identities on her social media accounts.

The phone rang, and she answered on the third ring.

"Ryan Morgan Commercial Reality." She listened to the reply, requesting to speak with Ryan Morgan. "I'm sorry, Mr. Morgan is in a meeting. May I take a message?"

She scribbled down the name and phone number, then hung up.

A half-hour passed when Ryan Morgan entered the office. He grunted a hello and immediately went to the back of the office, returning shortly later with a cup of coffee.

"Good morning." Melisa looked up at Ryan. "You looked tired. Late night?" She passed him a paper note with the information on the earlier phone call.

"No, just the usual evening." He looked at the note. "I wonder what they want."

"He sounded eager to talk to you. Are we on for tonight?"

Ryan paused before answering. "Well, I think we have to cool it for a bit. The wife is getting suspicious. You know how it is."

"Why won't you tell her you want a divorce, or at least a separation?"

"We've talked about this before. I don't want to pay her half of what I've earned. Be patient."

"I am, but sometimes I feel you're stringing me along."

"I don't want to talk about this right now." He went into his office, closing the door.

Melisa stared at the closed door for a moment. She sat her desk, cursing Ryan's name. Melisa typed a brief letter, printed it, and placed the paper in a courier envelope. She added a name and address on the envelope, placing it on top of the other courier items waiting to be picked up.

"You shouldn't lie to me, Ryan. Now you'll pay the price."

18

Friday, Late Afternoon

RACHAEL LOOKED UP FROM THE LIVING ROOM CHAIR WHERE SHE WAS reading a book. She saw Joseph carrying a duffle bag. "Don't be too long at the gym. We have dinner reservations."

"Of course." He stopped to give her a long kiss. "I'm looking forward to our movie date."

Joseph climbed into his SUV, let out a deep breath, and started the vehicle. He drove to the gym, carrying his duffle bag into the building. He used his card to gain admission past the turnstile and made a point of greeting the attendant behind the counter as he went past. He entered the changing room and sat on a bench, checking his watch. He opened a locker and placed his cellphone inside. He took a deep breath, preparing himself.

———

AN HOUR LATER, JOSEPH OPENED HIS LOCKER, BREATHING HARD. HE stepped out of the locker room and went to the front counter, asking to speak to one of the registered trainers available at the gym.

A few minutes later, a buff young man approached him. Joseph asked what his rates were and what were the expectations of following his advice. He exchanged business cards with him and left the gym.

————

MICHAEL SUTTON HELD HIS CELL PHONE IN HIS HAND, STARING AT THE screen. He leaned back in his armchair in his condo's living room. He took a deep breath, slowly releasing it. He touched the phone, activating the list of frequently called numbers. Next to Ryan Morgan's name was his mobile and office number. He chose the office number. He listened to three rings and a familiar voice answered, pleased the receptionist didn't answer. *That means she has gone for the day.*

"Hey, Michael, what's up?"

"Nothing much, but I'll be going by your office later and was wondering if I could stop by before you left."

"Sure, but I have a date tonight. Can't we discuss tomorrow morning at our golf game?"

"It's better we meet privately. A business situation. It'll only take a few minutes. Let's keep golf to casual."

"Okay, see you later. What time?"

"How about five?"

"Gripes. That's a bit late for a Friday, but I have some reports to do, anyway."

"Thanks, Ryan."

"Sure, see you then."

Michael put his phone on a table. He went to his kitchen and poured himself a glass of rum. He went over his plan in his head, deciding it was very doable. *The only missing ingredient is courage.* He looked at his drink. *Liquid courage.*

An hour later, Michael put down his cell phone on a table. He slipped on a windbreaker and patted the pocket where he kept the newly purchased knife. He checked another pocket where he had a few other items he needed to complete his mission. He exited his condo, going to the end of the hallway where the stairs were located. He went down the quiet cement stairwell, counting the floors as he went. He exited on the main floor and turned toward the fire escape door. Black letters warned an alarm would sound if opened.

From his pocket, he took a small magnet and attached a two-sided tape to it. Above the door was a white plastic box that met with a smaller one attached to the door. He reached above the door and attached the magnet to the white box. Next, he took out a roll of duct tape. He pressed on the door handlebar, slowly opening the door. The alarm stayed silent. He used a length of duct tape to cover the latch along the side of the door. He stepped outside, getting a look from two men sitting on the asphalt road as they leaned against a nearby brick wall. He ignored them and left the back lane, reaching the sidewalk that led to bars and shops. He spotted two taxis waiting at the curb and entered the first one.

He gave the driver the address, sitting behind the driver and kept his face turned to the side window. When the cab reached the destination, he passed over a twenty-dollar bill and exited.

After he stepped inside the building, he used the stairs to reach Morgan's office. He focused on keeping a steady pace to the office. He put on a pair of leather gloves as he walked. His hand shook as he reached for the door. Michael's memories vividly recalled the day a sobbing Brooke told him she was pregnant and decided to marry the father of her unborn baby. His anger rose, his hand stopped shaking, and he opened the door. The lights in the main office were off, but he saw Ryan's private office door was open with the lights on. It did not surprise him the receptionist wasn't there; Ryan had told him before Melisa usually left early on Fridays.

"Ryan, it's me." He stepped past the office door, not seeing him at his desk. He took another step and saw Ryan lying on the floor, face down. Bood soaked the back of his shirt. Blood formed a pool around his head from a cut at his throat. Michael stared at the body for several seconds.

Near the body was a safe, the door open. The inside of the safe was empty.

Michael walked backward, turned around, and hurried out of the office. He closed the door behind him and ran down the hallway to the stairs. He went down the stairs two at a time, reached the main floor, and used the rear exit of the building to enter the rear parking lot. Michael stood, trying to slow down his breathing and focus on what to do next.

Michael decided to follow through on his original plan. He walked down the back lane, tossing the unused knife in a dumpster two buildings down. At the next building, he threw away his gloves in another dumpster. From there he made his way to the street. After a few minutes, he hailed a cab, directing the driver back to his condo building. He paid cash for the fare and went to the back of the of his apartment building. He pulled open the rear door, removed the duct tape and the magnet, ensure the door was closed, and used the stairs to return to his apartment.

Inside his apartment, he threw away the remains on the tape and the magnet, putting them in a white kitchen bag. He carried the bag to the garbage chute in the hallway and returned to his apartment. *Done. I don't know who killed Ryan, but whoever did it did me and the world a huge favour.*

————

PAIGE STEERED HER CAR DOWN THE FAMILIAR STREETS, COMMENTING TO Brooke, "I had a nice lunch with Michael a few days back. You know, he blames himself for not proposing to you before he left that summer."

"That wasn't his fault. I don't know if I'd have said yes. I was still enjoying the free life. Our triangle was pretty good, if on the wild side."

"Then Ryan came along. That's okay. We all make choices and take chances. Some things work out better than others."

"I told off Ryan this morning. Told him I believed he was having an affair, which he denied. He also avoided explaining where he was hiding the extra money he was making. I sort of gave Ryan an ultimatum. I told him I want to try for another. He wasn't so sure, thinking a baby would interfere with our vacation plans. I told him I didn't care about that stuff and that we didn't need anymore money."

"What did he say?"

"You know. He's still in love with his money. There are times I could kill him."

Paige drove silently for a few seconds. "Well, if we were to kill him tonight, we'd have each other as an alibi."

Brook looked at her.

"Forget I said that. I'm sorry."

"That's okay. I'm not the type to kill anyone, regardless of the reason."

"I know that. You're a hippie child. Me, on the other hand, have no such qualms when dealing with two-timing jerks. Sorry, just thinking out loud."

"No need to apologize." She looked out the window. "We're close to his office."

"Hey, do you feel like sharing one of those cinnamon buns?" She pointed at Charmaine's Coffee Emporium, located across the street from Ryan's office building.

"Sure."

Paige swung the Jeep to the curb. She glanced at the building across the road, checked for traffic, and left the vehicle. She met Brooke on the sidewalk and together they entered the coffee shop.

"It's always busy in here." Brooke said as she stood in front of the glass counter that showed off various bake goods.

"These all look so good, but I'm still going with the cinnamon bun." She peered at the pastry with nuts and a golden syrup covering it. "And I don't want to share."

"That's something coming from you, who counts every calorie. I'll have one too."

The young man behind the counter appeared eager to take their order. "I'll bring the coffee to your table when it's ready." His grin showed his interest in the two women.

Paige looked at his name tag. "Thanks, Andrew."

Paige paid for the coffee and buns, taking the tray of the two pasties to a table near the back of the restaurant.

"He looked like he was ready to jump over the counter to serve you," Brooke commented.

Paige laughed. "Yes, he seemed enthusiastic about his job."

"So, tell me what's going on in your social life. You were seeing Char. What happened to her?"

"Uh, you know. She wanted someone who took care of her all the time. I want someone who can at least pay for her own drinks occasionally."

"I get that. What about men? They usually pay for dinner." She gave a teasing smile.

"Oh, no. The odd fling is okay, but men and I don't usually get along."

"Except for Michael. Both of you are unattached, and I know you and him can share a bed."

Paige laughed. "Right, hook up with a guy who's still in love with you? Problems galore there."

"True. I just wish for you and Michael to be happy." She paused as Andrew delivered the coffee. He lingered, asking how the food was.

Paige answered. "It's good, but we're in a rush. We have to meet our husbands soon."

Brooke looked at his retreating back. "Well, that scared him off." She grinned. "I guess with you wearing that short skirt and high heels, he had his hopes up."

"He's not bad looking, but acting cool is not his strong suit. Hey, I'll be back in a few minutes. I need to use the washroom."

Brooke took a bite of her cinnamon bun, tearing off a piece of the sticky pastry. She did a casual scan of the coffee shop. The customers were enjoying the coffee and food, and she continued to eat her pastry. Paige still didn't return from the washroom, and she wondered what the delay might be.

Paige returned to the table, walking quickly.

"That took a while." Brooke looked at Paige. "Are you alright?"

"Yes." She quickly sat. "Sorry, there was a line up at the washroom."

Brooke watched her quickly take a drink of her coffee and work on her cinnamon bun. She slowed down her movements and gave her a smile. "These are good."

They finished their coffee and pastries and exited the café. Paige opened Jeep's passenger door for Brooke. She walked around the vehicle, taking a long look at the building across the street.

Paige accelerated the Jeep out into traffic.

"That was fast."

"Yeah, sorry. Just lost my concentration for a moment." She frowned. "When I was in the washroom, I got a text from Char. She said a couple of nasty things."

"Sorry. I thought you were upset when you returned from the washroom. We can talk about it while we're having dinner at Joey's."

"No, let's forget about her." She forced a smile. "We can talk about what the future holds for us."

"What do you mean?"

Paige bit her lower lip. "I just want you to know, no matter what happens between you and Ryan, that I'll always be there for you."

"Okay. You know I love you too. What brought this on?"

"My spidey sense is tingling. I'm worried about how Ryan is treating you."

"I don't believe Ryan would ever get violent with me. He may cheat on me, but I'm safe from him hurting me physically."

"I'd beat him up if he did. But, let's say if he left you, disappeared, you call me first, alright?"

"Alright." Brooke reached over and squeezed Paige's hand.

19

Saturday Morning

MICHAEL LOOKED AT ROVER AND JOSEPH AS THEY STOOD BY THE clubhouse. "I wonder where Ryan is."

Rover grunted. "Late, even for him. I'll try calling him again."

"What did you do last night?" Michael asked Joseph while Rover called.

"I went to the gym and then took Rachael to dinner and a movie. That's all."

"Sounds like things are going well between you two."

"Yes, they are. Thanks for your advice."

"Great to hear things are now good with Rachael."

"Yes. That problem has been resolved." Joseph turned away and cleaned one of his drivers with a cloth.

Rover spoke up. "Still no answer."

"I'll call Brooke." Michael touched a few buttons on his phone. "Hi, Brooke, it's me. Do you know where Ryan is? He's a no-show for our golf game." He listened to the reply and ended the call. "Brooke doesn't know either. She's with Paige and is going to head home to check if he's there."

Rover frowned. "Maybe he's been in a car accident. If it's something serious, we should forgo the golf game and start calling hospitals."

"Agreed." Michael pointed to the sign that showed where the dining lounge was located. "Let's go there and make a few calls."

As they climbed the stairs to the lounge, Michael asked Rover, "What did you do last night?"

"Worked late to finish a roof. Better to have the crew work a few extra hours than to return on Saturday."

"You don't actually work on the roof yourself, do you?"

"Not usually. Just to help out if the crew is short staffed. I check on the progress from ground level. I just sat in the truck and made sure the job was finished, which means cleaning up the yard of any mess we made."

"So you sat in your truck for a few hours at the site?"

"I left to get a cup of java at Tim's." He smirked. "Tough life I live."

As they drank coffee, Michael received a call from Paige. He relayed the information to the others. "Ryan isn't there, and neither is his car. Paige is going to stay with Brooke while we try to find out what happened to him." He paused. "We should check his office."

Rover answered. "I'll try calling his office. If he doesn't answer, we could get the building security to check his office."

Michael put down his coffee cup. "I hope it's nothing serious." He looked at Joseph, who was studying his cup of coffee.

20

August 25, Saturday, Late Morning

Moss Stone arrived at the office of Ryan Morgan Commercial Real Estate. Anya Roberts, the medical examiner, and a uniformed cop were already present. "Great way to spend a Saturday." He looked at Roberts. "What's the situation?"

"In the next office, they discovered a Ryan Morgan this morning, dead. He was stabbed in the back and his throat slit."

"How was he discovered?"

"He failed to show up for golf with three of his buddies. He didn't answer his cell, and later they convinced the building security to check his office."

"Where's the security guard now?"

"Downstairs, waiting for you to talk to him. He doesn't normally hang around the building but works for a security firm that covers several buildings."

Stone headed toward the private office. "I guess he'll collect overtime pay a while longer." Stone looked around the office, noting the furniture all looked new and expensive. Next to the desk, Ryan Morgan lay on the floor, his blue shirt soaked in blood. One leg was drawn up, as if he was attempting to crawl. The pant leg smeared a trail of blood. Nearby, a heavy safe sat with an open door. Stone peered inside the empty safe.

"Looks like this is a violent robbery. Maybe there was cash in the safe." Roberts spoke behind him.

"Hmm. Blood money?" He bent his knees to look at the body closer. There appeared three distinct blood spots on his back and a blood line at the throat.

She frowned at his joke. "There's another factor in this robbery. Morgan is married, and the coroner estimated the time of death to be late Friday, likely after five. I'm wondering why his wife, or anyone for that matter, didn't report him missing yesterday."

"Good point. Perhaps his wife didn't expect him home, or maybe she's out of town."

"Or maybe she's the one responsible for his death."

"You don't have a good opinion of married women." He gave her a smirk. "Aren't you jumping to conclusions awfully fast?" He went to the desk and opened drawers. He used a pen to pick up a handgun. "Have the lab check this out if something has fired recently it or if the bullets match any unsolved shootings." He rummaged around and produced several flash drives, each labelled with two initials. He placed them in a bag and sealed it. "These might have something on them we can use. In fact, have his computer taken in and checked for contents. Where is the cellphone?"

Roberts held up a plastic containing a cellphone with a smashed face. "They found this under the body."

"Have the lab check it. It looks like someone wanted to destroy what was on it."

"Okay, anything else?"

"Yeah, why didn't he use his gun against any intruder? Maybe he knew his assailant and didn't expect an attack." Stone gave an opinion on his own question.

"Or maybe he didn't have time to get it. He was found dead by the safe and not at his desk." She pointed at where the body lay between the safe and the desk.

"True. And then there's the broken cellphone. It appeared someone wanted to make sure it wasn't useable anymore." Stone walked over to a credenza next to the safe. On top was half filled bottle of whiskey. He picked up the bottle and put it down. "It seems odd to have this just sitting here. It's possible he was having drinks with someone when the hostilities occurred. Let's interview the security guard."

They went downstairs, leaving the officer and coroner to remove the body and secure the office.

The guard was sitting behind a small desk on the main floor. The young man with black hair was working on his cell phone.

Stone showed him his identification. "Can you describe what you saw? Was the office door open when you arrived?"

"No, it was closed."

"Locked?"

"No."

"Lights on?"

The guard hesitated. "No, but I turned on the lights in the main office area. The lights in the next office were on."

"Good to know. Did you touch anything other than the front door and light switch?"

"No, but I was also wearing gloves." He held up a pair of black leather gloves.

"Are there any security cameras here? In the lobby, elevator, or even outside the building?"

"None. Old school security. The front door has a timer lock. After seven pm you need a pass card to get inside. The back door goes to a parking lot. You need a pass card to drive into the lot and to enter through the back door. There's also an underground parking lot. You also need a card to access it."

"Rather light security. Are there many problems here?"

"No. The offices here are all clients that don't have a lot of visitors. During the winter, we have to ask a few transients to leave. That's about it."

"Alright, you can go. We'll contact you if we have more questions."

Stone stepped outside the main doors, with Roberts following. He scanned the area. "See any cameras?"

"No. There's a coffee shop across the street. Maybe someone saw something from there."

They crossed the street, entering Charmaine's Coffee Emporium. Roberts showed her police identification, speaking with the brunette working behind the counter. "Were you working here yesterday evening?" She saw her name tag read Louise.

"Yup." She continued to fix a special-order coffee. "I was here, along with Marcie and Andrew. They'll be here again at three."

"Did you, or anyone, see anything unusual last night? Specifically, across the street."

"No, I wasn't really looking outside. We're busy from four to seven, so I'm just behind the counter."

"How about Marcie and Andrew?"

"I'll ask them when they arrive. They work the tables and may have a better vantage point." Louise glanced at Roberts and Stone. "Anything else?" She wiped the spigots for producing steam milk.

"Could I have a large dark roast to go?" Stone asked.

———

STONE AND ROBERTS RETURNED TO MORGAN'S OFFICE WITH ONLY THE COP present. Stone visited the inner office once more, studying the interior. He opened the closet door, seeing a few shirts, ties and two suit jackets. Stone went over to the window, pulling aside the curtains. The view wasn't enticing, showing a parking lot next to another brick building. He returned to the outer office, noticing the furniture was sparse but modern. He examined a name plate on the desk. "See if you can find out how we can hold of Melisa Regan." He opened the desk drawers, finding pens, two paperback romance books, lipstick tube, nail polish, and a hairbrush. "Not exactly a site of hard work."

He left the desk, going to the rear of the office. An open doorway led to a mini-kitchen comprising a coffee maker, a dishwasher and cupboards. Stone did a casual look over. "Nothing much here."

Roberts watched him. "I guess our next step is to see if Mrs. Morgan is home. I wonder how she'll react to her husband's death."

"Her reaction may tell us all we need to know."

21

Saturday Afternoon

ROBERTS LOOKED OUT THE PASSENGER WINDOW OF STONE'S CAR AS THEY approached the Morgan's home. "Nice neighbourhood. Expensive houses here."

"It seems our late Mr. Morgan has done okay for himself."

"I suppose, if one ignores the fact he was murdered."

Stone parked on the long driveway of the three-car garage. "Now for one of the nasty parts of the job, informing a death to a family member."

"A wife who didn't even report her husband missing. I wonder what her response will be when we tell her of his murder."

They walked up to the brick sidewalk to the front doorway. Moments later, an anxious looking blonde opened the door.

Stone introduced Roberts and himself. "Mrs. Morgan, may we come in?"

"Of course." She stepped to the side and followed them to the living room.

Roberts gestured to the leather couch. "Perhaps you should sit down."

Brooke nodded and sat. Her fingers interlocked as she looked at Roberts. "What is it? What happened to Ryan?"

"Mrs. Morgan, I'm sorry to inform you, they found Ryan dead this morning in his office."

She gasped, covering her face with her hands.

Stone stepped back as Roberts sat next to her. "Can I get you anything? Call someone for you?"

Brooke shook her head. "How did he die? Was it a heart attack?"

"No, we are treating this as a murder investigation."

"Murder? My god. What happened? Was he shot?"

"No, he was stabbed. Do you know of anyone who would want to do him harm?"

"Ryan has made a few enemies, I suppose."

"Anyone come to mind?"

She shook her head, mumbling, "Sorry."

"Alright. Didn't you find it unusual he didn't come home yesterday or last night?"

Brooke took several shallow breaths before answering in a broken voice. "Ryan sometimes stays out all night, so I wasn't concerned Saturday morning. I went out with a girlfriend last night and stayed there overnight. I was at her place when Joe called me that Ryan didn't show up for their golf game. I tried calling Ryan again and when I didn't get an answer, I drove home to see if he was here."

"Who were you with?"

"Paige Butler. She'll be here soon. When Ryan wasn't here, I called her and asked her to come over."

Stone walked around the spacious living room while Roberts asked questions. Expensive paintings hung on the walls along with high-end furnishings. He peered into the dining room and kitchen, satisfied the home belonged to a wealthy couple. On the granite countertop, he saw two empty wine glasses. He walked over to them, noticing lipstick was on both rims. He returned to the living room, where Roberts was still asking questions.

"I'm sorry for asking this, but how was your marriage with Ryan?"

"We were going through a bit of a rough spot. Nothing serious. He was working too much. Long hours. I wanted him home more."

"Was there an affair?"

"An affair? You mean with Ryan?" She frowned. "Maybe. I don't know for sure."

There was a knock at the front door and a woman hurried in. The dark-haired woman was wearing tight blue jeans and a fitted black top.

Stone focused his attention on her. "Excuse me. Who are you?" He held up his police identification.

"Paige Butler." She barely looked at Stone and went right to Brooke, who stood at her approach. "Brooke, what happened?"

"It's awful." Tears flowed again. "Ryan has been murdered."

Paige hugged her. "I'm so sorry."

Stone watched the two women hug. He looked at Roberts, who shrugged, and back at the women. They finally broke apart.

"I'll get you a drink." Paige walked to the kitchen with Stone following her.

"Were you with her last night?"

"Yes. All night if you need to know." She opened a kitchen cabinet door, revealing a wine fridge. She removed a bottle, twisted off the screw cap, and got two glasses from a wine rack.

Stone watched her pour the chardonnay into the glasses. "Were Ryan and her having marriage problems?"

She glared at him. "Seriously? Her husband was just murdered and you want me to gossip about their marriage?" She walked back to the living room carrying the glasses. After she handed a glass to Brooke, she turned to speak to Stone. "I think you should go now. Brooke needs some recovery time."

"Just a few more questions."

"Goodbye." Paige pointed at the front door.

Roberts nodded. "Let's go, Moss." She stopped to gather Butler's address and phone number. "We'll be in touch."

Paige stood at the front door, calling out as they walked away. "Call me first when you want to talk to Brooke again."

Stone turned. "Are you her lawyer?"

"No, her friend."

"Then we don't need to call you first." He turned and walked to his car.

"Please, as a courtesy."

"We'll consider it." His reply was directed toward where his car waited.

———

"THOSE TWO LOOK TO BE VERY CLOSE FRIENDS," STONE COMMENTED AS HE drove.

"They do. If Brooke was having marital problems, it would account for her needing a close friend for support."

"Yeah, I listened to your interview and caught the part where you asked about an affair. I thought Mrs. Morgan was under the impression you may have been asking if she was the one having an affair."

"I heard that too, but maybe it was confusion because she was distraught."

"Or it's possible because she was having an affair. There were two wine glasses in the kitchen from the night before with lipstick on both of them. Later, Paige told me Brooke spent the night with her—emphasising the entire night. Maybe they were more than just friends."

"Could be. But women do have sleepovers. It isn't always about sex."

"Okay, but I still think they're more than just girlfriends. They could have murdered Ryan, and each claim the other as their alibi." He smiled. "Maybe the Butler did it."

Roberts groaned at his joke. "The knife in the back shows it might be personal. Let's talk to his golf buddies in the meantime."

———

A FEW BLOCKS AWAY, STONE DROVE TO ANOTHER HOME. COMPARED TO Ryan Morgan's home, it was smaller, but still looked well maintained and modern in a well-to-do neighbourhood.

Stone rang the doorbell of the two-story home.

A woman peered from behind the front door.

Roberts held up her identification. "Mrs. McCarthy? We're looking for Joseph McCarthy? Is he available?"

"Of course. Please come in." She led them to the front room, calling out to the kitchen. "Joe, the police are here."

Joseph entered from the attached dining room, wiping his hands on a towel. "Hello, I was trying a new recipe." He held the towel for a moment and placed it on the back of a dining room chair. "Sorry, I wasn't expecting you."

Roberts nodded. "You and your friend were the ones who first reported Ryan Morgan missing and later contacted the building security. We just want to go over a few details with you."

"Certainly." He gestured to the furniture in the front room. "Please, sit down. Would you like a coffee or tea?"

Stone responded quickly. "Black coffee, please."

Roberts added. "Mine with cream, thank you."

Rachel walked to the kitchen. "I'll make it."

"What do you need to know? Ryan didn't show up for our golf game and we became concerned. After a few phone calls, we contacted the building security to check his office. The rest you know."

"We want to find out more about Ryan in the days before his death. As you may be aware, he was murdered." Roberts looked at his face, but it didn't change.

"Yes, we heard that from the security guard. He informed us he had called the police."

"Were you his closest friend? Did he have other friends?"

"I wouldn't call us close friends exactly, but I've known him for several years. He had other friends. Michael and Rover often golfed with us and attended a few social evenings together."

Stone accepted the coffee from Rachel. "Did he have other acquaintances? Perhaps some female friends?"

Rachel looked at her husband. Joseph answered. "I'm sure he did, but Ryan didn't tell us any names. He was part of our little group, which includes Rover and his wife, Lydia, Paige Butler and Michael Sutton."

"Michael, Rover and you were friends of his?"

"Yes, one could put it that way. To be blunt, Ryan could rub people the wrong way. We were his friends but were careful in our dealings with him." He looked at Rachel for a moment.

"Tell us more about Ryan. What did he do that made him unpopular?"

"He was unscrupulous, especially in business. He would cheat at golf, not counting all his strokes."

"Do you know if he had any enemies?"

"None that I know of, but that's certainly possible."

Roberts looked at Rachel. "Can you add anything about Ryan? How do you feel about him?"

"I have to admit, I didn't like him very much. He was arrogant and didn't care about others." She glanced at Joseph.

"Yet Joseph and you were friends with him." Roberts took a drink of her coffee.

"We have a history together." She took a deep breath. "Michael, Brooke, Paige, Lydia, Joe and I all went to university and hung round together. We have stayed friends, but like family, you don't always like what a person does."

"Rover wasn't part of the university group?"

"No, he married Lydia later."

"How about Michael and Paige? Are either of them married?"

"No. Michael just hasn't found the right woman yet. And Paige, well, she's gay. Now that doesn't mean she can't get married to a woman, but she hasn't found the right partner yet."

"Okay, just one more thing. Where were you and Rachel Saturday night?" Stone closed his notebook.

Joseph looked at Rachael. "I went to the gym and then we went to dinner and then a movie."

"That sounds nice. Fancy restaurant?"

"Normand's on Jasper. We've been there before."

"It is nice. They have wild game on their menu. What movie did you see?"

"The Empty Motel. It's a horror show."

"I heard about it. Tell me the best scene."

Rachael spoke. "That would be when the creature enters a room from under the floorboards. It comes up behind that poor girl and, well, I better not spoil it for you."

"What time did you go to the gym?" Stone asked.

"Hmm, it was a bit after four when I arrived there. I guess I was there for an hour. After I finished, I talked to a trainer." He checked his shirt pocket, producing a business card. "You may keep it." He passed over the card to Stone. "You can also check my cellphone. The GPS will show I was there for a full hour."

Stone pocketed the card and stood. "Okay, thanks for your help."

————

ROBERTS ASKED, "WHAT ARE YOUR IMPRESSIONS OF THEM?"

"They sure act nervous about something. When a couple keeps exchanging glances, it can mean they're hiding something. And Joseph was a little too forthcoming on his alibi at the gym."

"Yeah, but that doesn't make them killers. Besides, they went to a dinner and a movie that night. It's new, and she did describe a scene in the movie, so it seems she did actually see the movie."

"We should check the time of the dinner reservations. Maybe it was murder, dinner and a movie."

22

Saturday Afternoon

STONE PEERED AT THE BUNGALOW FROM THE CURB. "NICE LOOKING HOME. Not in the same price range as the Morgan's, but this is higher than a detective can afford."

"You spend your money on your bike, so it's time to re-evaluate your priorities."

"My bike isn't the problem. As any guy can tell you, girlfriends are expensive."

"It's the bike." Roberts closed the car door.

They walked up the sidewalk and rang the doorbell. "Okay, partly. But girlfriends are still expensive."

"You're lucky she puts up with you."

Rover Driscoll opened the door.

Stone looked up at the big man, showing his police badge. "Can we come in? We're investigating the death of Ryan Morgan." He noticed tattoos on both arms.

"Sure," he growled out the word. Rover pointed to the front room, calling out to his wife. "Lydia, the police are here to ask about Ryan."

A brown-haired woman entered the room. "It's awful what happened. I can't imagine what Brooke is going through." She gave a brief smile. "Tea or coffee?"

Stone replied, "Black coffee, please."

"Tea for me," Roberts answered.

Stone watched Rover ease into a cloth armchair. He gave Stone and Roberts a hard look. "How can we help you?"

"We're looking into the murder of Ryan Morgan. We're hoping you can shed some light on who would want him dead and why." Stone accepted a coffee from Lydia after she gave Roberts a tea.

Rover grunted. "There are lots of reasons someone could be angry with him. Who would actually kill him? That I can't answer."

"What are the reasons?"

"Ryan was a liar and a cheat. He also didn't respect the vows of marriage."

Lydia spoke up. "Rover, don't speculate. Remember, Ryan had good qualities as well."

Stone asked, "What do you mean by not respecting vows of marriage?"

"Have you met his secretary?"

"No."

"He didn't hire her for her typing."

Stone nodded. "How do you know he's a liar?"

"My own dealings with him. I invested money in his bar. He lied to me about business expenses, making up stories about a flood and needing to repair the cooler. So I wasn't getting any return on my contribution, but he sure didn't seem to suffer from a lack of funds."

"That sounds like a motive for murder."

"No. Rover has given himself to the Lord. He would not commit such a sin." Lydia spoke firmly.

Stone looked at Roberts and returned to Rover. "Well, I can appreciate a commitment to one's beliefs, but would you have an alibi for Friday night?"

"I was at work until after five, grabbed a bite to eat, and went to the church to do some repair work."

"Where do you work?"

He gave a grunt of annoyance. "I own a roofing company. I do little physical work myself, but I check up my crew and see if there are any problems."

"Is there anyone who can vouch for you at the worksite or the church?"

"My work crew saw me at the site. I was alone at the church."

"Rover, is that a nickname?"

"Yeah, if you must know. I played rugby when I was younger. The name stuck."

"What's your real name?"

He hesitated and frowned. "Matthew."

Stone and Roberts left, returning to his car. Stone drummed his fingers on the steering wheel. "What do you think? Killer or not?"

"He sure looks like he could be one. Tough-looking guy. But according to his wife, he couldn't do such a thing."

"Well, she wouldn't be the first wife to protect a husband who committed a crime."

"True. Shall we check up on the receptionist? Or Michael Sutton?"

"Let's go and visit the receptionist. Perhaps she'll be less grumpy than Mr. Driscoll."

"He didn't seem to enjoy our company. Maybe he's always rough around the edges."

Roberts placed a call to Melisa Regan.

Stone listened to the conversation, frowning when it ended. "So, she doesn't want to meet us today."

"She said she was on her way out for an appointment. But she said we could see her tomorrow."

"It's possible there's something in her apartment she doesn't want us to see and needs to remove it. Like a knife."

"Could be, but we can ask her questions tomorrow. Perhaps there's another reason she doesn't want us to see her place, or she actually has an appointment she can't cancel."

"Let's visit Michael Sutton instead. He also lives downtown." He looked at Roberts. "Can you call him first?"

"Sure." She listened to her cell phone. "You don't like talking on the phone, do you?"

Stone shrugged. "I prefer face-to-face communication."

————

THE CONDO BUILDING ENTRANCE FEATURED A SECURITY GUARD SITTING behind a counter. At his eye-level sat a pair of monitors.

Stone introduced Roberts and himself as police, informing the heavy-set guard they had an appointment with Michael Sutton.

"No problem." His eyes glanced at a monitor. Seconds later, a steel door opened, and a couple emerged carrying shopping bags.

"Do you have a lot of cameras?"

"Mostly in the parking lot. We've had a couple of break-ins in the past and beefed up our security there. This is the only way in and we have twenty-four hour security here."

Stone nodded and proceeded to the elevators with Roberts. They rode the elevator to the thirty-fourth floor, where they exited, turning left down the hallway.

Sutton stood by his open door. "Come on in, detectives."

The apartment had modern furniture but with a minimalist style. Roberts sat in a black swivel armchair while Stone walked around the condo on the thirty-fourth floor, impressed with the view. He slid open the balcony doors and stepped outside. From his vantage point, he could see the North Saskatchewan River twist through the banks of the river valley. He returned to the condo. Michael eased himself into a loveseat, watching Stone.

"Very nice spot you have here. You must do well in your business consultation."

"It's been good."

Stone looked at the kitchen, small compared to the rest of the apartment. He studied the high counter that separated the kitchen from the living area. The granite surface held an angry cartoon figurine swinging a golf club at a post. A caption underneath stated, 'I play golf for fun'. An empty tumbler sat in the middle, and at the far end a metal platter held unopened mail and several coloured dollar bill sized coupons. Stone recognized the Canadian Tire money that carried various nominations of five cent to a dollar. He calculated the amount on the tray to be fifty cents. "How do you like living downtown? Is it hard to get around?" He sat in an armchair identical to Roberts'.

"No, I can walk to most places around here. If I feel lazy, I can have groceries delivered. Just about everything I need is within a few blocks of here."

Stone joined Roberts on the couch. "We understand you were a friend of Ryan's."

"Yes, I've known him since university. There is a group of us that met back then and stayed in touch. Later, marriage added to the group."

"When was the last time you were in contact with him?"

"We played golf together last weekend. Joseph and Rover were there as well. I talked to him the day he died on the phone that afternoon. It was a brief conversation."

"What was it about? Did he sound stressed?"

"I just asked him if he wanted to carpool for the golf game. He told me he would have to drive alone as he had to take care of some work first. I can't say he sounded any different than usual."

"What was he like? Did he have any enemies?" Stone glanced at Roberts as she was taking notes. He saw her sketch a symbol she used to portray calmness with a question mark after it. He looked at Michael, who held his hands together across his stomach.

"He was okay with me. Ryan and I joked around a bit. Back in university we hung around a lot. What was Michael like? He was, to be blunt, a bit of a weasel. He ran a few different businesses and some of them sounded shady. You know, flipping real-estate, pyramid schemes. Rover invested money into a bar Ryan had a partnership in. Ryan was never hurting for cash, but that bar lost money, or so he claimed. Rover was pretty upset with what was happening."

"Did Rover threaten him?"

"I don't know. I would guess, yes. Rover has a short fuse. He did some prison time for assault. Thing is, Ryan was married, but didn't act like it. I suspect there are a few jealous husbands and boyfriends who would like to have a word with him."

Roberts stopped writing. "Yet you considered him a friend?"

Michael shrugged. "I'm not married and free to play around. If I was married, I would make it plain I better not catch him alone with my wife."

"In your group of friends, was Ryan taking an interest in someone's wife?"

Michael pursed his lips. After a few seconds, he responded. "Perhaps, but I don't want to speculate. Ryan looked at every woman as a potential bed partner. So, just because he was interested in someone, it doesn't mean the attraction was reciprocated."

"Fair enough." Roberts looked at her notes. "Now, we need to ask, where were you on the night Ryan was murdered?"

"Here."

"Can you prove it? Any witnesses?"

"You can check the building's security log. It'll show I arrived at the parking garage just after four. I entered the building shortly afterward. I didn't leave until the following morning. The security log will prove I never left after arriving here that night."

Stoned asked, "Just one exit for the building? No other exit?"

"There's a fire exit at the back. As far as I know, the door is alarmed. I've never used it. I believe it goes to the back lane."

Roberts made another scribble in her notebook. "So, there may be jealous men out there. What about women? Did he break the heart of a woman that may want to seek revenge?"

"It's possible. None of the women I know. Lydia is religious and spends a lot of time at church functions. She's certainly not violent. Nor is Rachel. She's a quiet woman. And Paige is a lesbian. I doubt Ryan would have much success with her." He gave a grin.

Roberts and Stone thanked Michael for his time and waited for the elevator.

"What do you think of Michael as a suspect?" Stone jabbed the elevator button a second time.

"Everything he says sounds reasonable. He acts calm. But..."

"But...?"

"It was almost rehearsed. There weren't any stumbles in his answers. People when they lie often have twitching fingers. He held his hands together and never separated them. I find that a bit odd."

"I noticed he claimed he could do all his shopping within a few blocks of his condo. I saw Canadian Tire money on the kitchen counter and the closest Canadian Tire is a mile from here. He didn't really lie there, but he wasn't entirely forthcoming either."

The elevator arrived and Stone was quiet as the car made its descent.

Roberts poked him in his ribs. "What's on your mind?"

"I'm just thinking about what Michael said about Ryan. It sounds like Ryan was a dirtbag, doing sleezy business deals and screwing around with as many women as he could find. He likely has a few people happy to see him dead."

"That may make it harder to pinpoint our killer."

"I suppose. But it makes me curious why his wife hadn't given him the boot."

"Maybe they had an open marriage. Or maybe she was planning a divorce but hadn't involved lawyers yet. Some women don't give up on a marriage, no matter how bad it seems to others."

Stone shrugged. "What we know is the Ryan Morgan was a piece of work. A liar, cheater, womanizer and had a lack of scruples. He was stabbed in the back multiple times, and again in the throat. The safe was emptied. This looks like a murder of a personal nature, and the robbery was a bonus."

"That could be true. I say we call it a day and meet in the office tomorrow. By that time forensics may have more information on the time of death and the lab may decipherer the contents of the computer and cellphone."

23

Sunday

Stone wandered into the quiet office in the downtown police building. On a Sunday, traffic of vehicles and people was light, and he entered the office area from the elevator, heading to the coffee room. He yawned as he poured a coffee, turned and walked toward his desk. Stone saw Roberts was already working at her desk that faced his own. He strolled over and eased himself into his chair, leaning back as Roberts opened files on her computer. He slurped at his coffee, getting a frown from her. "It's hot."

"Then wait until it cools down."

"What do those files on Morgan's computer show?"

She clicked a few keys. "Not surprisingly, he kept two sets of accounting books. His bar was making a tidy sum according to a second set of books. On another set, it shows high expenses and much lower sales, barely breaking even."

"That would make Revenue Canada unhappy, but I doubt they

would kill him for that. But our friend, Rover, might not be under the same restraints."

"His wife is adamant Rover wouldn't go against what the Bible says."

"Yeah, well, maybe he closed the book for an hour."

Roberts moved on to another file. "Old photos. University student days, it looks like."

Stone stood and went to her desk, peering over her shoulder. He saw a group of six people sitting on a lawn, recognizing a building in the background as part of the University of Alberta. "That would be Joseph McCarthy, Lydia Driscoll, Ryan Morgan, Paige Butler with long hair, Michael Sutton and Brooke Morgan. Notice, Michael has an arm around the waist of Paige and Brooke? He looks like the cat that caught two canaries."

"And Ryan is standing by Lydia. It appears like Michael was close to Paige and Brooke at one time."

Roberts clicked on a few more photos, some taken during a party, concerts, and camping. Most of the photos showed Michael with Brooke. A few showed Brooke and Paige together. Rachel McCarthy appeared in a few of them, each one with Joseph close by her. It reminded Stone of the carefree days of youth, and he said so. "Those were the days before we had to worry about responsibilities like paying bills."

"True, but sometimes it feels good contributing, too. Hey, here's a pic of Ryan and Brooke together, and another." She went through a few more. "Wedding photos." She pointed at a Brooke in a white dress. "That's a baby bump."

"That may explain the wedding."

"It looks like Joseph is the best man and Paige and Lydia are bridesmaids. No sign of Rover or Michael in these pictures."

Stone pointed at another photo of the wedding reception. "There's Michael sitting with Paige at a table. Neither looks too happy."

"The wedding looks subdued. A lot of people, but there doesn't appear a lot of dancing." She opened another folder. "Oh, my."

Stone stared at the nude photos of Brooke. "Nice looking woman."

She closed the file. "Nothing wrong with having nude photos of a spouse."

"Yes, but some spouses look better than others."

Roberts sighed and opened another folder. "You should look at these photos as a professional..."

Stone saw the images of Rachael, her arms secured by a rope behind her back. Her face was filled with emotion as she stared at the camera. She opened a few more photos, all showing Rachael nude and tied up. "If Joseph McCarthy found out about these photos, we just might have found a motive for murder."

"Maybe he was blackmailing them." Roberts closed the file. She hesitated and opened another folder named MR. A blonde posed nude and in black leather outfits. Another series of photos showed her on a dancer's pole.

"I wonder if MR stands for Melisa Regan."

"The receptionist."

"If so, it would be an interesting employer-employee relationship."

"I'm sure." She opened the next folder, labeled PB. The nude photos showed a young woman lounging on a bed. Some photos were of the tease variety as she held up a blanket to partly cover herself.

"That must be Paige Butler. Long hair, but that's her."

"These photos must have been taken during their university years. Ryan Morgan sure has quite the collection of nude women. It could be related to his murder."

She opened another folder, marked JC, revealing images of another woman in various stages of undress. "I wonder who she is."

"Pretty girl. Perhaps someone he was going out with. I wonder if there are more photos on his cellphone, the ones the killer wanted to destroy."

"That could be. Let's hope our lab can recover what was stored in it." Roberts looked at a message icon on her computer, clicked on it, and read the message. "The lab has checked the gun. There are partial fingerprints that match Morgan's, but there are another set that don't belong to him. What's really interesting is the gun was unloaded. No bullets. He also doesn't have a permit for the gun."

"Why would Morgan keep an empty gun in his desk? That's hardly a recipe for protection."

"The fingerprints don't belong to him. Possibly, someone emptied the gun so he couldn't use it."

"Or he bought the gun without bullets and hadn't purchased the ammo yet. If he was careful in touching the gun, the fingerprints may belong to whoever he purchased it from." Stone looked at his watch. "Time for a coffee. Maybe on our visit to Melisa Regan, we'll get some more answers about Ryan. I wonder what her reaction will be about those photos of her. Maybe she'll give us more information on his friends and enemies."

———

THEY DROVE DOWNTOWN, REACHING A NEW HIGH-RISE THAT GAVE A VIEW of the river valley. Stone parked in a no-parking zone and lowered his visor, showing he was on police business. They entered the front doors and used the intercom to gain access to the lobby after speaking to Melisa Regan.

Stone pushed the eighteenth-floor button, riding in silence until the car doors opened. "Judging by the lobby, it looks rather expensive to live here."

"And she does it on a receptionist's salary," Roberts gave a sarcastic reply.

"Perhaps she's frugal in other ways."

Melisa opened the door, giving a broad smiled as she invited them in. "I guess you want to speak to me about Ryan. It's just horrible." She indicated a white leather couch for them to sit. She directed her question at Stone. "Can I get you a coffee or tea?"

"Sure, black." He looked at the well-dressed woman. Short grey skirt, light-blue blouse, jewellery, well-done hair and makeup. Each fingernail was done in two colours. "Were you planning to go out?"

"Just to my hairdresser." She glanced at Roberts. "Black as well?"

"With cream."

After Melisa disappeared into the kitchen, Roberts whispered, "She's dressed like that to go to her hairdresser? Does her hair even need a cut?"

"So she likes to look good. What of it?"

"Nothing, except it makes me suspicious of her."

Melisa returned, passing a coffee mug to Stone first and then Roberts before sitting in an armchair across from them.

"How long have you known our victim, Ms. Regan?" Stone asked.

"Please, call me Melisa. I've known Ryan for about a year and a half."

"Were you the receptionist during that time? Or did you know him prior to that?" Stone took a drink of his coffee. He looked around at the modern furnishings. On a wall behind her chair hung an oil painting. On the wall behind the couch hung a similar, larger painting. Past the living room, a marble counter indicated where the kitchen was located.

"Office manager. I met him shortly before. We got along and he offered me a position at his firm."

"Correct me if I'm wrong, but. you were also his only employee."

"Yes, Detective Stone." She frowned. "What is your first name? It sounds so formal to call you Detective Stone."

Roberts interjected. "Do you know if Ryan Morgan had any enemies? Someone he may have had an argument with?"

"I guess he didn't get along with everyone. I suppose that's the nature of doing business."

"Names? Examples of arguments?" Roberts snapped out the questions before taking a sip of her coffee.

"Well, this woman had a meeting with him and there were a lot of loud words. She called him a bastard."

"What was her name?"

"I don't know. Tall, slim. She had short, dark hair. She had an attitude. Wait, I think it was Paige."

"Okay, anyone else?"

"Yeah, there was this big guy. Tattoos on his arms. He told off Ryan, said something like 'or else'. He didn't look very friendly."

"No name?" Roberts held her pen poised over her notebook.

"No, we didn't keep a visitors' book, and Ryan used his own method for booking appointments."

"Do you know what he kept in his safe?"

"No. He kept it locked. I guess it was for important papers."

"I think that's a safe assumption. What was your relationship with him? Were you friends, or more than just friends, with him as well?"

"Yes, we were friends. We actually went on a few dinner dates. I told him, since he was married, I didn't want to get into a serious romantic relationship with him." She paused and licked her lips. "Ryan told me he wanted to divorce her, that their marriage had broken down. He believed she was having an affair. She wouldn't agree to a divorce unless he gave her a lot of money. At one time, he wondered aloud how expensive it would be to have her knocked off. I was shocked, and he dropped the subject. Maybe she decided to strike first."

"What were the normal office hours? Nine to five? What time did you work to?"

"Our office hours were nine to four. Ryan usually came in around ten."

"Short work day for him."

"Ryan would work late, usually until six. It was the nature of his business. Often, he would work late, have dinner and meet clients."

"Do you know anything about a bar he owns?" Roberts scribbled in her notebook.

"I know he owned a bar, but he did little with it as far as I know. I think it was just a tax write-off."

Roberts looked at her notes. "We found photographs of you on his computer. Would you care to elaborate on them?"

Melisa smiled. "I'm also a model and do freelance work. I normally charge a lot for those kinds of photos. But for Ryan, I gave him a special deal. A friend discount." She looked at Stone. "I'd like to be your friend."

"Okay, if you think of anything else, give us a call." He passed over his business card.

They left the apartment and headed to the elevator.

"She sure was quick to name others who may have a grudge against our victim," Stone commented.

"Including Mrs. Morgan, who she claimed was the one having an affair. With her pointing fingers at so many others, it makes me wonder if she is the one who we should be investigating. I don't believe she doesn't know what was in that safe. Small office and she goes on a dinner date with him. She knows more about him than she's saying."

"You may be right. But I'm having trouble picturing those skinny fingers with long nails using a knife to kill him. A gun, yes."

"So, she's innocent because of a manicure? She pointed one of those manicured fingers at his wife. And what sounds like Rover Driscoll and Paige Butler." She paused. "She would be a dangerous friend."

"She's not the type of woman a man could be just friends with. Siren would be a better description of her."

"I'm glad you see her that way. She sure was flirting with you."

"Yeah, likely to throw her off as a murder suspect, which has the opposite effect."

"We might as well call it for today. We can continue tomorrow. By that time, we should have the autopsy results."

"I agree. It'll also give me time to think about the clues and the people involved."

"Number one suspect?"

"Hmm. The man with the great alibi and calm demeanor. Michael Sutton."

"I'm going for the wife. I think she hired someone. What are your plans tonight?"

"I'm going to catch up with Cindy. She worked until three last night, so I didn't get to see her."

"Say hello for me. See you tomorrow."

———

Moss Stone reached the condo building where Cindy lived, carrying a large paper bag. She opened the door for him, giving him a kiss.

"Thanks for bringing dinner. I'm starving."

"Cheaper than going to a restaurant." He grinned. "And I don't have to pick out the wine." It surprised him to see her wearing a shimmering black dress and high heels.

Cindy laughed. "It's better if I pick out the wine, truth be told."

"You're right. I'd likely order a beer instead. You look great."

She opened the bag and pulled out the containers. "Thank you." She gave him a long smile. "Padmanadi's is so good. I love their food." She placed the food onto individual plates.

"You know, part of the advantage of takeout is not having to use dishes."

"Let's pretend we're civilized. Open the wine. It's in the fridge."

Moss sighed and retrieved the wine. He read out the label, "Chateau Langlois Saumur Chenin. That's a lot of words for white wine."

"There's white wine and there's white wine. This one, a chenin blanc, has high acidity, which works well with spicy foods."

"Okay, I'll take your word for it." He poured the wine into glasses and carried them to the dining room table. He took a drink of the wine. "Not bad."

"I'm glad it meets with your approval." She grinned as she set the plates on the table.

They divided the food and ate.

"Tell me about your latest murder. How's the investigation going?"

"Just starting. The victim was stabbed in the back and his throat slit. Someone didn't like him. His safe was also emptied, but we don't know the contents of it."

"Did he have a lot of enemies?"

"Yeah, there are a few that are glad to see him gone. He was screwing around on his wife, so it's possible she got rid of him. Or maybe a jilted mistress. Or a jealous boyfriend."

"But he was also robbed."

"There is that. Maybe the robbery was the original intention, and he became a casualty. Or, he was the target, and the robbery became a bonus."

"I would say the back-stabbing means it was personal. The throat-slash may have been the finishing touch. That's a horrible thought. That would mean he really pissed off someone. Any leading suspects?"

"No, not yet. Alibis are all good at first look, but we'll poke at them, and something will not quite add up." He refilled the glasses. "This wine really is good. Goes well with the food."

"And the food?"

He put down his fork. "Okay. I'll admit the food is good. Damn good."

"See, vegan food can be good."

"I don't disagree. It just seems a lot of work to make vegetables taste like chicken."

"You're hopeless."

"By the way, Anya says hi."

"Thanks. I'll text her hello later. Does she have a theory on who the murderer is?"

"Yeah. She suspects the wife, who claims she was with the girlfriend that night. He was cheating on her, but I would've thought a gun would be more her style. A knife attack can go wrong, especially since he was bigger than her."

"You have a point. Women are more devious than men when planning a murder. Still, a back-stabbing could be considered poetic justice to a cheating husband. Anyway, she was with her girlfriend, so they would both have to be in on it."

"From what I saw, they were very close girlfriends. Our victim also had nude photos of the girlfriend. Both women had a reason to want to get even with him."

"For what it's worth, I suspect it was a man who murdered him. A knife attack is something a woman would avoid, partly because a man is usually physically stronger. A gun, or poison, is a better choice for a woman.

"Since he was stabbed in the back, perhaps the killer had to strike there because he was smaller than the victim and wanted to use a surprise attack."

"How big was the victim?"

"Average height. Good point on wanting to use a surprise attack. Stab in the back first and then slit the throat. As far as suspects, one is a woman who knows martial arts. All the men are big enough to consider using a knife."

"On that happy thought, do you want more food? Otherwise, I'll put the leftovers in the fridge."

"I'm stuffed."

Anya cleaned off the table. "Go sit in the living room." She finished the wine bottle into the glasses.

Stone took his glass to the living room, sitting on the stylish, but uncomfortable, loveseat. He waited for her to join him, admiring her figure and her dress at her approach.

"This is great. Just you, me and the wine."

She sat next to him. "It's been a while since we've had a proper date."

"It has been. You're a busy girl and my days off are when you usually work."

"I really enjoy our time together. You know you're the only one I'm seeing, don't you?"

Stone shifted on the coach. "I assumed so, but we never officially said it was a monogamous relationship. For the record, you're my one and only."

"Good, because you have a lot more free evenings than I do. If you're testing the waters, let me know."

"My boat is tied up at the dock."

She kissed him. "Then that's settled." She finished her wine. "Turn on the TV and find a movie or something." She stood and went to the kitchen, returning with another bottle of wine.

"Are trying to get me drunk?"

"You're not a lightweight when it comes to drinking."

"Yes, but I do have to work tomorrow morning. You know, the murder case?"

"Moss, that's tomorrow's problem." She filled his glass.

"But I have to drive home."

"No, you don't. If you can't guess already, you're spending the night here."

"I'll drink to that."

———

STONE SLOUCHED AT THE KITCHEN TABLE, WATCHING CINDY, WEARING ONLY a long t-shirt, make coffee. "I don't know which looks better on you, the dress or the t-shirt. Both have merits."

She gave him a mug of black coffee. "Toast and eggs?"

"No thanks. I'm too tired to eat."

She sat across from her with her own cup. "What are you thinking about?"

"Do you remember a while back when we met Anya at the Local Public Eatery?"

"Yeah, that's when I met her."

"I remember you saying something like, 'Moss and his coffee.' How did you know I like coffee so much? Like, usually when we go out, we have drinks, not coffee."

"What's your point?"

"I'm curious if you met Anya before, and she told you of my fondness for coffee. Because, how else did you know about my coffee addiction?"

"Hmm. Let me phrase it this way. You come here for dinner. We have wine and spend the night together. In the morning, you accuse me of secretly meeting up with Anya in my free time to talk about you. Is it possible that your super smart girlfriend observes how much coffee you drink when you have a chance, such as the time we had breakfast at De Dutch restaurant?

"So, which way are you leaning? The super smart girlfriend or the one that sneaks around and has meetings with your partner?"

"I'll go the super pretty and super smart girlfriend."

"Good choice."

"I better get moving." He stood. "I'll call you later."

———

CINDY WAITED A FEW MINUTES AFTER HER GOODBYE KISS WITH STONE AND then called Anya.

"Hey, Moss spent the night with me. I need to tell you he is suspicious we met before."

Cindy listened to Anya's reply, and the replay the morning conversation.

"It's all good now. I just wanted you to know."

24

August 27, Monday Morning

ANYA ROBERTS LOOKED AT STONE AS HE MADE HIS WAY DIRECTLY TO THE coffee room. She returned her thoughts to her monitor as she studied the reports.

Stone came up behind her. "What do we have here?"

"Autopsy on Ryan Morgan. According to this, the three stab wounds were not the cause of death. The knife used had a short blade and didn't penetrate deeply. Eventually it could have led to loss of blood and death, but none of the punctures themselves hit a vital organ. Death occurred from the throat being slit. It appears to be a different knife used to cut the throat. There's one other injury. A blow to the head just above the left temple. The coroner believes the blow was strong enough to either knock him out, or at least render him stunned. She speculates the victim was first hit on the head, either by an object or a fist, and then stabbed in the back. At this point, he may have been left for dead."

"So perhaps a second attacker entered the office and finished him off."

"Could be. The coroner estimates fifteen to thirty minutes between the backstabbing and the throat being slit. It could be two different perpetrators, or the same one. Perhaps, after emptying the safe, the victim showed signs of life and the attacker finished him."

"So, after stabbing him in the back, the perpetrator slit his throat. Why would he, or she, use a different knife?"

"Possibly two different attackers, but they were working together."

"That complicates things."

"I was thinking of Brooke Morgan and Paige Butler were together that night. Both had reason to be angry with him. Two women. Two knives."

"Good point. We need to talk to them again. They spend a lot of time together, so we need to interview them separately and find a gap in their alibi."

"We also have information on the crushed phone. They retrieved the memory and extracted more photos. They were the same as on the computer and flash drives."

"How was the phone broken? Were there any impressions on it, like a shoe marking?"

"No, whoever did this, likely used the edge of the heel. We have the log of messages and phone calls."

"Good, print that out and let's see if there's something there."

"Okay, done. How was your evening with Cindy last night?"

"Good. We had takeout at her place. How was your evening?"

"Quiet. I stayed home and watched TV." She walked over to the printer, picking up two copies of the cellphone calls and messages. "Not many calls during that day, but a few messages." She quickly scanned the printout. "Those messages are for doing a rendezvous and are for something other than business reasons."

"That doesn't surprise me, from what we've been told about him. Let's check out who is on the receiving end of the phone numbers and messages."

Roberts handed him the sheet of paper.

"You start." Stone scanned the sheet. "I need another coffee."

"What a surprise."

Stone refilled his coffee cup, phoned Cindy, and returned to where Roberts was working. "Anyone interesting show up on the phone messages?"

"No surprises. He received a call from Michael Sutton earlier that day, but that just confirms what Sutton said before. Just the usual texts. He was setting up a time and place with a woman for Saturday. Her name was Jill Campbell. He sent her a few texts last week as well."

"Jill Campbell. Maybe those are her photos listed under the initials J C. Okay, let's do search on the internet on our suspects and see if anything interesting turns up." Stone sat at his computer. "I'll take Brooke, Michael and Paige. You check Rover, Joseph and Rachel."

"Okay, I'll also do a search on our victim. We may find more clues there."

STONE RETURNED FROM THE COFFEE ROOM AND SAT IN FRONT OF HIS computer. "I'll tell you what I got. Not too much on Brooke Morgan. She does some charity work, works on a couple of boards to help the homeless. She graduated with a bachelor of science. Hmm, it seems she lived a quiet life. Not much on Facebook. Her girlfriend, Paige, on the other hand, has a busy life. A few different jobs since she left university. She took business courses that gave her a job as a waitress, a ski shop clerk and now as an instructor at Women's Whole Body Gym. Lots of images of her on her Facebook page and advertising her services at the gym."

"What about Michael Sutton?"

"Not much on social media. He has a low-key website advertising his services as a business consultant, whatever that entails. He has a LinkedIn profile. Looks professional, but I can't find much else on him. In any case, no criminal record on any of my three suspects."

"My suspects are a bit more interesting." Roberts swivelled her chair to read from her monitor. "Rover Driscoll has a criminal record. Drug possession, assault, robbery, and resisting arrest. The assault record includes the use of a knife in a bar fight and assaulting a police officer. After his last infraction four years ago, his record is clean. Not even a speeding ticket. His wife doesn't have near as much information, other than photos of her at a church function. She is the church secretary, and her image appears at a lot of their charity functions.

"Joseph and Rachel McCarthy are rather quiet, according to the internet. She works for the government. He sells oil field supplies. Not much going on with them."

"What about our victim?"

"A few things. The real estate board has fined him a few times for questionable practices. He shows up on a few golf tournaments, charity auctions that feature high-priced items. From what I see, it looks like he's a high-roller.

"His receptionist, or office manager, as she likes to be called, has quite the profile on Facebook, Twitter, Snapshot and anything else on social media. She has a members only site, and I think that alone tells you how she makes a living."

"Then why the office manager's job? That seems odd." He clicked the top of a pen a few times as he listened to Roberts.

"I think it's a method to meet rich clients."

"Good point."

"Okay, now what do we do next?"

"I say we interview the two girlfriends. How about I take Paige Butler and you take the grieving widow? We interview them at the same time."

"Okay, but let's bring them here rather than going to their place. Let's make them nervous."

"I'll pick up Butler. When I have her on the way downtown, I'll call you and you can get Brooke Morgan."

———

STONE ENTERED THE WOMEN'S WHOLE BODY GYM, STOPPING AT THE reception desk and requesting Paige Butler. He received a few looks from the women entering the lobby. At the entrance, several posters advertised various classes. One poster headlined Paige Buttler, instructor for a self-defence course. A few minutes later, Butler appeared.

She stared at Stone. "What are you doing here? How did you know I work here?"

"I'm a detective, remember?" He noted her yoga outfit. "Do you want to change? I'm taking you downtown for an interview."

"Am I under arrest?" She glared at him, snapping out the words.

"Not yet."

"This is bullshit." She turned and strode toward to locker room.

"Ten minutes." He phoned Roberts, informing her to pick up Brooke Morgan.

Fifteen minutes later, Stone escorted Butler to his car.

"This is a police car?"

"What can I say? I march to a different drummer."

She got into the black, three-door Veloster. "Maybe you march to a whole different band."

He started the vehicle and made his way downtown.

"Why downtown? You could ask me questions at the gym."

"We have our reasons. One of which is if you confess, we have you close to the holding cells."

"I didn't kill anyone. I don't have a confession to make."

"Then you have little to worry about."

She crossed her arms. "You're a bit of a jerk." She watched him shift the gears. "A police car with a standard?"

"I enjoy driving. My other vehicle is a Harley."

"You are different."

"What do you drive?"

"A Jeep Wrangler."

"So we both drive unusual vehicles. I say we have something in common."

"Yeah, we both like women."

Stone laughed. "There is that."

"Is this Police 101, where you try to get the suspect to relax by having a rapport with her?"

"No, I'm just conversing with you. I doubt anything I say will get you to like me. But that's not important. All I want is to find the killer of Ryan Morgan."

"Then you're looking at the wrong place if you think I did it."

"I hope you understand I can't take your word for it."

———

Stone parked his car and escorted Butler to the elevator. After arriving on his office floor, he offered her something to drink.

"I know that routine. It's so you can get a sample of my DNA from whatever I drank."

He held open the door to the interview room. "There's no DNA in this case. No weapon has been found. Nothing to go on but perfect alibis from all his friends."

"Tea with milk."

"Okay. Make yourself comfortable."

Stone went to the coffee room and returned to the room, seeing her sitting on the edge of the table.

"How does one make oneself comfortable on metal chairs?"

"Good point. Durability is the key here. No budget for comfort." He passed her the tea.

"Thanks." She sat on the chair.

"Okay, in Police 101, I'm supposed to establish a rapport with you. I'll ignore that. Another tack is to accuse you of killing the victim and watch your reaction. I doubt that is going to work." He took a drink of his coffee. "But I will go with this. My partner has Brooke Morgan in another interview room. You claim to be with her that evening, so let's see if your stories corroborate.

She sighed. "This tea isn't very good."

"You should have gone with the coffee. What time did you meet up with Brooke?"

"I finished work at two. I went home, changed, and drove over to her place. Maybe half-past three at that point."

"What did you do there?"

"We drank some wine, talked, that sort of thing. An hour later, we left in my Jeep and headed to the bar to eat dinner."

"What bar? What did you eat?"

"Actually, we stopped at a coffee shop first for a coffee and a cinnamon bun. Then we went to Joey's at South Common. I had fish tacos and Brooke had a burger."

"Who paid for the meal?"

"I did. Cash. The server was Suzz." Paige spelled out the name. "She was nice, jet-black hair. She'll remember us."

"Brooke has more money than you. Why did you pay?"

"She usually pays for our outings. But I told her she was my date, so I paid."

"Your date? Does that mean something?"

"It does. It meant I would take care of her. She was feeling anxious, so I wanted to comfort her."

"Then you went to your place?"

"That's right. More wine and more talking."

"Did you talk about Brooke divorcing Ryan?"

"Yes, but Brooke also said she wanted to get pregnant with him again. She wanted to try to have a baby."

"What did you say to that?"

"It's her choice to make. You likely wouldn't understand, but when a woman gets the urge to have a baby, it overrides a lot of other things." She took a drink of her tea. "If you think Brooke would want to kill Ryan, that makes zero sense if she wants to get pregnant."

"Another man could get her pregnant."

"That's not how Brooke thinks. She's been loyal to Ryan despite his lack of commitment. No way was she considering another man."

"Okay. Tell me about university. I saw photos of Brooke pregnant when getting married to Ryan."

"That was a tough time." She stared at her tea.

"How so?"

"Michael, Brooke and myself were friends with others, but us three had a special relationship. We called ourselves the delta group."

"Delta group?"

"The Greek symbol for delta is a triangle. We formed a triangle.

Michael was going out with Brooke. I was, let us say, friends with both of them. During the summer, he went to work in Prince Albert. While he was away, Ryan moved in. He got Brooke drunk a few times. By the end of summer, she was pregnant, and accepted his proposal."

"Michael must have been upset."

"Yeah, he was. I know you think that may have been a motive for murder, but that's not how Michael does things. He's a fixer. He should've been a councillor. Michael finds a solution to problems. Here, he remained friends with Ryan, so our group could still be together."

"One might think eliminating Ryan is a solution for Brooke."

Paige shook her head. "If Michael were to kill Ryan, that would put an end to their relationship. Brooke is a lovely person, totally non-violent. She would have nothing to do with Michael if he were to murder Ryan."

"Okay, so does that mean he would murder Ryan if he believed he wouldn't get caught?"

"Michael isn't that devious. I know him." She leaned back.

"You're quite certain of him. Do friends know everything about their friends?"

"Maybe not. But Michael and Brooke are my best friends. We were really close at university and stayed close over the years. I know him."

Stone looked at his notes. "Were you aware there were nude photos of yourself on Ryan's computer?"

"Yes. He showed them to me."

"Under what circumstances?"

Butler sighed. "He asked me to come to his office for a business proposition. I met him and he showed me the photos."

"Was that part of the business proposition? Was he going to blackmail you?"

"No. He just wanted to show me he had them. He made it seem really sleezy. I don't care he had the photos. Just the way he showed them to me."

"They were old photos."

"Yup, during my university days. I needed some money, so I did the photo sessions. They ended up in some men's magazine." She shrugged.

"So what did this have to do with the proposition?"

"He wanted me to be an escort for a client of his. The client was a woman, also gay."

"So, in exchange for keeping the photos secret, you had to be an escort?"

"That was his thinking. But I've had more photos done since university. I really don't care if someone sees them. I like my body."

"Did you escort his client?"

"Yeah. He also gave me five-hundred bucks. The thing is, if he had simply asked me to help him out at this dinner meeting, I would've said yes. I didn't like him, but I try to help people when I can. Besides, being an escort is something I can tell people when I'm old and grey."

"Something to brag about, alright."

"If I were to guess, you've done things that are best told only after a few drinks."

"Okay, you got me there." He shifted in his chair. "To summarize, the nude photos meant little to you, but the five-hundred dollars was the enticement."

"Sure. He only pissed me off by showing the photos. And no, I wouldn't kill him for that. Beat him up, perhaps, but that would be it."

"I saw your credentials at the gym. You ever need to use those skills?"

"No, but I feel better knowing I can kick ass if someone gives me a rough time."

"Alright." He stood. "Another tea?"

"Sure."

Stone went to the coffee room, refilling his coffee and making another tea. He returned to the interview room, dropped off the tea, and proceeded to the next room. Stone tapped on the door and entered, beckoning Roberts to follow him outside. He saw Brooke Morgan, looking distraught as she sat.

"How's your interview going? Brooke Morgan looks upset."

"She is. She can't believe we think she had anything to do with Ryan's murder. Every time I tried to talk about him, or who may have wanted him dead, she began to cry. If she murdered her husband, I'm sure she left tears at the crime scene."

Stone summarized his interview with Paige Butler. "The end result is, she claims Brooke, and herself had drinks, went to a coffee shop, dinner and end up going to her place. We can check out the restaurant and confirm they were there and the time."

"I'm getting the same story from Brooke. I'm getting cool to the idea of those being the murderers."

"I agree. Shall we let them go?"

"Might as well. Brooke knows Paige is here. I guess she sent her a text when you picked her up."

"Okay, I'll finish up with Butler and have her sent home. Damn, I was hoping we had genuine suspects, but it seems they're not the ones."

He entered the office and sat.

"This is seriously weak tea."

"Another reason to drink the coffee."

"Do you still consider Brooke and myself as suspects?"

"Everyone is a suspect until we find the killer. But to answer your question, you're not number one right now."

"Who is?"

"I can't tell you that. He was stabbed in the back. It sounds personal to me."

"Ryan was an asshole. He had more enemies than just our local group."

"Likely you're right. But we have to start with those closest to him. Our clues are a knife attack and an empty safe."

"Empty safe? There was money in it before when I was there."

"What did you see?"

"Envelops with elastic bands wrapped around each one. Ryan took out one envelop and took out the five-hundred dollars. There were lots of envelops."

"See anything else?"

"No, just the envelops with the money."

"Was the safe locked?"

"No. He just turned the handle and opened it."

"Hmm. That changes a few things." He stood. "Okay, thanks for your help."

"That's okay. You're not so bad for a cop. But stop looking at Brooke as a killer. She just isn't capable of murder."

"Okay. Are you?"

"No, I'm all peaches and cream." She smiled.

"Who teaches martial arts."

"That too."

Stone escorted Paige Butler out of the interview room. "Time to take you back to work and save you from drinking more of our tea."

"Let me see Brooke first."

Paige embraced Brooke.

Stone saw Roberts looked skyward. "I'll have an officer drive you back to work."

After Brooke and Paige left, Stone informed Roberts on what was in the safe and compared interview notes. "She implied there was a lot of money in the safe."

"Maybe the murder resulted from a robbery, and not just revenge."

"Or a bit of both."

"Did Brooke indicate there was anytime they were not together?"

"No. They had wine at her place, then went for coffee, then dinner and finally at Paige's apartment."

Stone frowned. "If we remove Brooke and Paige as suspects, who do we focus on next? I say Michael Sutton."

"Well, I asked Brooke about her pregnancy. She said she was stupid to allow Ryan to seduce her with drugs and booze. When she became pregnant, Michael offered to marry her, but she decided it was best to for the baby to be with the father, Ryan. After they married, Brooke lost the baby. It sounded like after that, Brooke went into a depression. Anyway, there had to be bad feelings between Ryan and Michael. But she said that if Michael had anything to do with his murder, she would have nothing to do with him again."

"That just means he would have to murder Ryan without being caught."

"That means you want to have another visit with him."

"I do."

25

Monday Afternoon

THE SAME SECURITY GUARD FROM LAST TIME WAS BEHIND THE DESK AS Roberts and Stone entered Sutton's apartment building. The guard recognized them.

"Are you here to see to see Mr. Sutton again?"

"Yes," Stone replied, "but could you let us see the rear exit first? I understand it's a fire exit."

"Yes. It's also alarmed, so it's not used as an exit." He stood and placed a well-used paper sign on his desk. It read, 'Back in five minutes.' "I'll show you the way."

They followed the guard past twin steel doors, down a hallway with concrete walls, through another steel door that opened to a storage area. At one side wall was a door labeled 'Stairs' and at the far end was one more door. Yellow letters warned the 'Alarm will sound if Opened'. Near the door, a glass cabinet showed green lights.

The guard pointed. "That's the fire alarm control box."

"Does the door alarm work, or are those just words to prevent someone from opening it?"

"The alarm works." The guard opened the cabinet door and toggled a switch. "No point in having the alarm bells go off. They're loud." He pushed open the exit door and one of the green lights turned to a blinking red. "It works."

Stone looked at the red light. "Okay, and the alarm is loud enough for you to hear at the front?"

"Without a doubt. I also get a warning light on a console."

Stone stepped outside, looking at the back lane. He saw the usual dumpsters and walked to the end of the asphalt lane, seeing a pair of taxis parked along the curb. He returned to the building. "There must be a bar close by, judging by the cabs waiting nearby."

The guard confirmed his speculation. "Yup, a couple of restaurants and bars. A good enough reason to make sure this door stays closed."

"Okay, thanks. We'll just take a look around."

"Sure." The guard toggled the switch again and used a key to reset the alarms. The green lights returned.

After the guard left, Stone pointed at the top of the exit door. "See those two white blocks? Reed switches. The magnet in the block attached to the door prevents the alarm from going off."

"Rather simple. Door opens and the reed switch is activated."

Stone looked around and found an empty five-gallon pail. He carried it over to the door, turning it up-side-down and stood on it. He took out his cellphone and turned on the light, peering at the white block. "These blocks have been touched recently. The dust on them have been wiped off."

"Someone was tampering with them."

"Yeah, likely taping a magnet to the reed switch, so when the door is open the alarm wouldn't go off." He stepped off the bucket. "Want to look?"

"I'll take your word for it. Heels on a plastic surface are not a good combination."

"Let's call it in and get fingerprints off the exit door and the one to the stairs."

"By 'Let's call it in' you mean me."

Stone shrugged. "You're better on the phone than me."

"BS." She used her phone to place the call.

Stone returned the plastic pail to where he found it. He waited until Roberts finished with her call. "Shall we have a visit with Michael Sutton?"

"Sure. The fingerprint experts will be here soon. They'll also swab for DNA samples."

"Let's use the elevator. The stairs are too much of a challenge unless one needs to avoid being seen."

"You think Michael Sutton used the stairs up and down? Thirty-four stories? He must be in good shape for that."

Stone pushed the button to call for the elevator. "He may have used the elevator to travel from his floor to the second. The one thing he would want to avoid is getting off on the main floor where he would be seen by the guard or video equipment."

"So you think he is the murderer?"

"I'm not sure yet if he is the murderer. He doesn't strike me as the killing type. But I'm sure he's lying to us when he said he was in his condo all Friday night."

They entered the elevator and Roberts looked at him. "Usually, you have some theory in your head about a murder, something about the universe being connected, or some weird quantum physics approach to solving the murder. So far, you have offered nothing but facts. What gives?"

"I was thinking of chemistry. There's a natural bonding of elements that are very stable. For example, a water molecule. Two hydrogen atoms and one oxygen. H-two-O. It's a happy little triangle of atoms. But let's say another atom comes along, let's say sulphur, and takes the hydrogen away. Then we two unhappy oxygen atoms and an unstable hydrogen-sulphur bond."

"You mean Michael, Brooke and Paige were a happy triangle and then Ryan comes along and steals Brooke away."

"Exactly. From what I've gathered is Brooke doesn't want to hurt anyone's feelings. She's willing to put up with the sleezy behaviour of her husband because she doesn't like the thought of divorce. Brooke's not happy, but won't do anything to change it. She keeps contact with Paige and Michael. That fuels their desire to eliminate Ryan and go back to their happy triangle."

"Brooke said if Michael had anything to do with Ryan's murder, then she wouldn't have anything to do with him afterward."

"Yeah, but look at it from Michael's viewpoint. He knew Brooke was unlikely to get a divorce, no matter how bad it became in their marriage. He's still in love with her. So if he murders Ryan and doesn't get caught, the perfect murder, then Brooke will be free to join him and Paige again. If he gets caught, then at least Brooke will be free of Ryan and be happy again. A sacrifice, but a win for his love. And there's always a chance Brooke will forgive him later."

"Interesting theory. What about Paige? Does the same apply to her?"

"It does, but she was with Brooke all evening. That would mean both had to be involved in the murder." The elevator doors opened. "Paige is a martial arts expert. She could attack and kill Ryan in a minute. Maybe they weren't together every minute that evening."

"Possible. Let's see if Michael is our man."

Sutton opened the door, allowing the detectives to enter.

"What can I do for you this time, detectives?"

"Just a few more questions," Stone replied.

Sutton retreated into the condo and went to a chair where a coffee cup sat on a neighbouring table.

Stone remained standing after Sutton sat in an armchair. Sutton joined his hands together with his arms resting on his lap.

"Tell me, did you read that in a book on how to look calm while being interviewed by the police? Because I have to tell you, it looks a little too calm," Stone asked as he faced him.

Michael straightened up and unclasped his hands. "It's a force of habit. I deal with a lot of high-end businessmen, and one has to look calm, sincere and in control while dealing with them."

"Okay, fair enough. Can you tell me where the knife is that you bought from Canadian Tire is? You know, the one from the hunting section of the store?"

His jaw dropped.

"What? Surprised I figured that out? Where is it? In a dumpster?" He held up a pair of handcuffs. "Anything to say before we arrest you on murder charges?"

"I didn't kill Ryan."

"I guess I wasn't really expecting a confession."

"You don't have any proof I did. None, because I didn't kill him."

"Right. But I bet I can prove you bought a knife from Canadian Tire for the sole reason to murder Ryan Morgan. Stand please. Hands behind your back."

"I'll call for a car to take him in for booking." Roberts used her phone to place the call, looking at the anxious face of Sutton.

"Come on, your ride will be waiting downstairs."

"Call my lawyer, Levi Hurley. This is a mistake."

"Right. Pardon us if we don't take your word for it."

They took the elevator to the main floor, where two uniformed officers took Sutton away.

Roberts asked Stone, "What was with a knife being bought at Canadian Tire? I saw his reaction. It looks like you nailed it."

"Last time we were at his condo, I saw Canadian Tire money. They give that stuff when you pay cash or used a debit card. He already said he could get everything he needed downtown within walking distance. I wondered what he bought at Canadian Tire that he couldn't buy at the stores close to him. One thing is camping and hunting supplies. Canadian Tire has that, including hunting knives. Now we just need to find that knife."

"I hate dumpster diving."

"So do I. Let's ask for some blue shirts to investigate the area of Morgan's building, checking at least a block in all directions for the knife."

"What do we do? Go and question Sutton?"

"Let's join the search for the knife. Hopefully, it will be more supervisory than climbing into the bin."

"I'm wearing heels and a skirt. It won't be me going into the garbage bin."

"I'm wearing a suit."

"Tough luck."

———

Stone stood with Roberts as two officers removed green bags from a mustard-coloured bin. It was the fourth garbage bin they had investigated. Suddenly, an officer stood inside the bin, holding up a knife in a gloved hand.

"Great." Stone took the knife from him, sealing it in a plastic bag. He noticed the blade was clean, looking brand new. "Now, could you look for a pair of gloves tossed inside there as well?"

The officer said nothing. He gave Stone a long stare and bent to examine the bin again.

A few minutes later, the officer raised his arm, clutching another knife, this one smaller than the first. The blade was covered with what looked like dried blood.

Stone muttered sarcastically, "Great, two knives. Does that mean we're looking for two killers?" Stone retrieved the second knife. "Let's have a conversation with Michael Sutton. One of these knives is likely one of his, possibly both."

———

Sutton was sitting in the interview room when Roberts and Stone entered. They sat facing him from across the table.

"I'm not saying anything until my lawyer arrives."

Stone shrugged. "So be it. Then I'll talk. We found the knife you threw away in the garbage bin. Do you still want to insist you were in your apartment on the night of the murder?"

Sutton stared at Stone.

"Okay, have it your way. The longer you refuse to talk, the more time we have to build up a case as you the murderer. At a certain point, you won't have any bargaining power against the maximum sentence."

Roberts instructed the officer standing by the door to place him in a holding cell. "Call us when his lawyer shows up." She looked at Stone. "Do we just wait?"

"No. We're going to the closest Canadian Tire store."

———

STONE AND ROBERTS ENTERED THE BRIGHTLY LIT STORE, REQUESTING TO see the store manager when they stopped at the customer relations desk.

A few minutes later, a man in a sports jacket arrived. The slim, middle-aged man didn't appear to be surprised at their appearance. "How can I help you? Shop lifting problem?"

"No, this is a bit more serious," Stone explained. "We want to confirm the identity of someone who purchased a knife here." Stone opened his phone and showed the images of the two knives.

"I'll need to get our sporting goods manager to confirm this, but I believe we sell the larger knife. The smaller one, that's covered with blood, is not one I recognize as being available here." He turned to the clerk. "Ask Kelly Richard to meet me at where we keep hunting knives."

They followed to the manager to the sporting good section, passing tents, coolers, kayaks and assorted camping gear. They arrived at a vertical stand with sliding, locked glass doors. The peg board showed various knives, ranging in size, quality and price.

A blonde woman approached them. "Hi, I'm Kelly Richard. Do you need information on these knives?"

Stone showed her his identification and the photos of the two knives.

"We sell the larger knife. The other knife, I doubt it is used for hunting. The blade is too small."

"Do you sell a lot of knives?"

"It varies according to the season." She did a mental calculation. "This month we sold around forty knives."

"You would have to unlock the cabinet for each sale. Do you think you'd recognize a photo of a customer who bought one of these?"

"Maybe. If they look like an adult, I rarely pay much attention to them."

Stone showed her a photo of Sutton on his cell phone. "Do you recognize him?"

"Hmm. Yes, I think so. Good-looking guy. He was well-dressed. I can't be certain, but I think he was here."

"To buy a knife?"

"Likely. There aren't many other reasons I would have to deal with him, besides guns. Guns require more than just money to buy. You also need a permit."

They thanked her for her help, getting her contact information.

Stone and Roberts left the store.

Roberts commented, "Too bad she couldn't be more positive in her ID of Sutton. I didn't know hunting knives were so popular."

"There're a lot of hunters out there."

"Obviously. Are we going back to interview Sutton, assuming his lawyer has arrived?"

"Yep. Maybe we can use the manager's statement to pressure Sutton."

———

THEY RETURNED TO THE POLICE HEADQUARTERS, FINDING SUTTON AND HIS lawyer waiting for them in the interview room.

Levi Hurley spoke. "We were curious how long you would keep us waiting." The lawyer slowly sat, opening a notebook as he did so.

Stone sat on a chair opposite on the table from Sutton. "Your client didn't want to speak to us earlier, so I didn't feel compelled to return at his convenience."

"My client maintains his innocence. I don't see where you have any evidence that justifies holding him."

Stone looked at Sutton. "We believe we can prove Mr. Sutton lied to us when he claimed to be in his apartment during the evening Ryan Morgan was murdered. He left his apartment by using the rear exit of the building and used a taxi, or another form of transportation, to arrive at the office of Ryan Morgan. There, he murdered our victim and returned to his apartment. He left a knife in a garbage bin. That knife was purchased at a Canadian Tire store.

"We believe we have sufficient proof that is the chain of events, and we are prepared to charge Mr. Sutton with murder."

Hurley tapped his finger on his notebook, studying his notes. He looked up at Stone. "Do you have any witnesses to the alleged movement of Mr. Sutton?"

"We have a possible identification at a Canadian Tire store where he purchased the knife. We will interview taxi drivers and Uber drivers later. One or more drivers will identify Mr. Sutton."

"But, so far, you do not have an identification. Your witness at Canadian Tire is not what I would accept as firm proof he purchased a knife there. Frankly, you don't have any proof. Just conjecture. Any witnesses you may produce of having seen Mr. Sutton on the night of question will only be able to give a vague description of a male. You know, I can tear apart any testimony your witnesses may have."

Stone looked at Robert, who gave him a frown. "If your client continues to insist that he was in his apartment that night, it means he was lying. We will prove he left his apartment that night."

"Perhaps, but not yet. I believe you have insufficient grounds to hold my client."

Stone sighed. "Advise your client not to make any travel plans." Stone stood.

Sutton and Hurley stood as well.

"Wait." Roberts looked at Sutton. "You can claim your innocence, but we know you haven't been truthful with us. So right now, you can go. I will tell you what we will do as soon as you return to your apartment. One is we will look for more clues about what you did that night. The other thing we have to do is to talk to Brooke Morgan and inform her we have a suspect in her husband's murder but cannot make an arrest yet." She paused. "I wonder how she'll react when she learns the suspect is you."

"You wouldn't do that."

"Why not? You lied to us and we're going where the clues lead us. She deserves to know her friend is a murder suspect."

"Can I have a moment alone with my lawyer?"

"Sure." Roberts left the room with Stone.

"Nice thinking there," Stone commented.

"From what our interview with Brooke and Paige told us, Brooke would never forgive Michael if he murdered Ryan. I think he wants to make a deal with us."

A few minutes later, Hurley signaled for them to return to the room.

"Against my advice, Mr. Sutton wants to make a statement."

Roberts and Stone looked at Sutton. They sat, and Roberts told Sutton to speak. "Go ahead. Just make sure it's the truth this time."

Sutton pursed his lips, took a deep breath, and spoke. "On that Friday, I gave Ryan a call to ensure he would be in his office. I told him it was a business situation I wanted to discuss privately. I picked 5:00 p.m. because I was pretty sure he would be alone by then. His receptionist usually leaves after lunch. He didn't hire her for her work ethic."

"So you arrived at his office at five?" Stone asked.

"About that time."

"With the knife?"

"Yes. Look, I wasn't sure if I would use it. I felt I needed a weapon. If Ryan would not listen to reason, I was prepared to do what I had to."

"Okay. What happened when you arrived at his office?"

"I opened the door to his office. The main lights were off, but the light to his office was on. I called out to him, but there wasn't an answer. When I went into his office, I saw him, dead, in a pool of blood."

"Why didn't you call the police if you didn't kill him?"

"I panicked. I wasn't sure if the killer was still close by. I didn't have my phone with me, although I suppose I could've used the land line in the office. My thought at the time was just to get the hell out of there."

"Do you recall if the safe was open?"

"Uh, yes. The door was open. The safe was empty."

"Did you notice anything unusual?"

"No, I just left as fast as I could."

"The next day you pretended you didn't know Ryan was dead."

"Right. I'm sorry if my actions caused a problem in catching the killer."

"Are you sure about that? Because one of your friends may be the murderer. Perhaps you were hoping that he, or she, gets away with it."

"I hear you, but I'm telling you the truth. And I know nothing more than that."

"Okay, you are free to go for the time being. You are still in trouble for lying to the police."

"I understand. But you won't tell Brooke you believe I'm the murderer, will you?"

"No, but we also won't be telling her you're above suspicion."

Sutton nodded. "Again, I'm sorry for not being honest in the first place." He stood. "If I remember anything else, I'll contact you."

Roberts looked at Stone after Hurley and Sutton left. "Do you believe he was telling the truth this time?"

"Well, I don't think he killed Ryan. That knife from Canadian Tire doesn't look like it had been used, unlike the smaller knife. As far as telling the truth, possibly he hasn't told us everything." Stone walked to his desk.

"I agree with you. That leaves with one less suspect if Sutton didn't do it. Who do we check out next?" Roberts joined Stone, walking to their desks.

"He claimed he didn't see anyone when he went to Morgan's office. Perhaps he saw someone and isn't saying anything to protect that person. We know he's very close to two women, Brooke and Paige." Stone sat at his desk, tapping a pen on his notebook.

"Let's interview Brooke again tomorrow. I want to know if there were even a few minutes when they weren't together Friday night." Roberts stood by her desk. "Are you going to inform Paige Butler we're going to question her? Remember she asked if she could be present if we talked to her again."

"Yeah, I remember. Let's call her when we arrive at Brooke's home. I wonder how long it'll take her to get there."

"So is that it for today?" She pushed her chair against her desk.

"I thought that we could go to Normand's on Jasper and confirm the McCarthy's did have dinner there."

"Okay, let's do that. Want me to call first?"

"That would be good. Hopefully, they won't be busy yet."

———

STONE PARKED HIS CAR ON JASPER AVENUE, A SHORT DISTANCE FROM THE entrance to Normands's restaurant. He checked for traffic on the busy road before opening his door, meeting Roberts on the sidewalk.

"Shall we go for dinner?" he asked lightheartedly.

"Only if you're buying. And I get to choose the wine."

"What is it with women that don't trust my judgement in wine?"

"Do you know what a Chablis is?"

"No. Some sort of a grape?"

"It's a Chardonnay from France, usually unoaked. I think you should stick to picking out beer."

Stone held open the door for Roberts, and they entered Normand's. A big man in a white shirt greeted them and Stone quickly identified themselves as police detectives.

"Good to meet you. I'm Normand. Follow me to my work area."

Stone and Roberts followed Normand to the upper level of the traditional styled restaurant. Near the entrance to the kitchen, Normand went to a table with chairs. "How can I help you? Would you like a coffee?"

Stone readily agreed to the offer of coffee. "We are checking if a couple had dinner here last Friday, Joseph and Rachel McCarthy."

"I can check." Normand went toward the kitchen, returning with two cups of coffee. "Sit down while I look at our reservations book." He held a black-covered book and opened it.

Stone saw his finger trace down the pencil writing to an entry.

"Here it is. I remember them now. They had a table at the front, by the window. Their reservation was for six, and it appears they arrived about that time."

"Excellent coffee," Stone remarked. "Anything unusual you noticed with our couple?"

"I wasn't their waiter, but I seated them. They acted like they were on a wedding anniversary. Holding hands, giving each other a kiss. They seemed happy. The gentleman spilled his wine glass, which we refilled for him."

"So was he nervous?" Roberts asked.

"I suppose, now that you mentioned it. I presumed it was jitters of an important date."

Stone thanked Normand for his help and the coffee. "I'll have to come back here for dinner soon."

Stone left with Roberts. "Damn, it smells good in there. I was ready to have a steak dinner."

"I'm sure you could eat a steak. But back to our case. The McCarthy's had dinner here, but it sounds like Joseph may have been nervous about something."

"Something like murder."

26

Tuesday Morning

PAIGE OPENED HER FRONT DOOR TO MICHAEL. "WHAT IS IT? YOU SOUNDED upset on the phone." She stared at him. "You better come in."

He went past her and stood in the living room. "Sorry, when I called you yesterday, and found out you were with Brooke, I knew I couldn't say anything."

"Brooke and I were wondering why you called and wouldn't say why." She stood close to him. "What's wrong?"

"That Friday, the day Ryan died, I went to his office late that afternoon." He paused. "I had a knife with me."

"Jesus. You murdered him?" She took a step back as she drew in a sharp breath.

"No. I was either going to kill him or beat him to a pulp. But he was already dead. The police arrested me, accusing me of murder, but they had to release me due to lack of evidence. I confessed I was there on Friday and saw his body, but I didn't do it."

"Slow down. Why were you going to kill him?"

He licked his lips. "It was the only way. I had to save Brooke from him. Ryan was into some nasty shit. Gangs were paying him to sell drugs in his bar. He was having an affair with Rachael. The man was without scruples. I decided to see him on Friday, intending to kill him."

"Michael, that's crazy."

"I didn't think I'd get caught." He sighed. "I'm not as smart as I thought I was. But even if I was caught, Brooke would be free. I know you'd take care of her."

Paige stepped forward. "Oh, Michael." She hugged him. "Please never do anything so stupid again."

"Alright, that was a dumb move. I wasn't thinking straight. I guess revenge was on my mind from what he did."

"For Rachael?"

"No. When he seduced Brooke."

"That's a long time to carry a grudge."

"I was okay with it for a while, but what he was doing to Joe and Rach, that was too much. My anger at that sleazy son-of-a-bitch came back." He sat on the couch and looked up at her. "What do I tell Brooke? Do I tell her I was planning to kill Ryan?"

"Well, before we discuss that, I have a confession to make as well."

He stared at her. "Has this something to do with Ryan?"

"Indirectly. I was at Charmain's, the coffee shop across from the building Ryan worked in. Brooke was with me. When I was there, I saw you through the window. You got out of a cab and were wearing a windbreaker. You usually wear a suit, and the way you were walking to the building, I knew you were up to something. I had a sudden feeling you were going to kill Ryan, and it scared the hell out of me."

"I had no idea anyone saw me."

"I did. I couldn't tell Brooke. It made me really anxious."

"I guess I caused problems for you. Sorry."

"That's okay. You wanted to do the right thing. But, Michael, killing someone is never a solution. If Brooke ever found out..."

"I know. But I had to save her from Ryan. I would go to hell for her."

"That may be true. But have you considered what Brooke wants?" She pursed her lips and continued. "Brooke still loves you, Michael. She wants you to live your life, not sacrifice it. Don't do what you think she may want. Stay true to who you are. That's the Michael, Brooke and I love."

He nodded, then covered his face with his hands. "I got tunnel vision. I saw Ryan as a problem that had to be removed, not as someone who needed help."

"Ryan was beyond help."

"Yeah, I guess so. But I never considered that option."

"Michael, there's always another option."

"Tell that to the man who is at the edge of a cliff."

27

MOSS STONE SAT AT HIS DESK, REVIEWING HIS NOTES ON THE RYAN Morgan murder. "I just don't like the fact there were two knives used in his murder, but we found only one knife that was obviously used. The other knife was brand new, and according to Michael Sutton, never used. That leaves another knife unaccounted for."

"More dumpster diving to find it?" Roberts replied.

"No, at least not yet. The knife may have not been thrown away. Like it may be a knife the killer keeps with him, or her, all the time."

"Do you still want to visit Brooke Morgan?"

"I do. The wife of the murder victim is always a good suspect, plus the fact she seems to have an unusually close relationship with Paige Butler."

"Okay, I'll call Brooke Morgan and confirm she's home."

"Good. I'll grab a coffee to go."

STONE PARKED HIS CAR IN FRONT OF THE MORGAN RESIDENCE. "OKAY, GIVE Ms. Butler a call and let her know we are going to have a talk with her girlfriend."

Roberts called Paige Butler, putting the phone on speaker mode.

"Hello."

"This is Detective Anya Roberts. We are going to interview Brooke Morgan. As a curtesy, we're letting you know."

"Thanks, but Brooke already called me. I'm on my way."

Roberts ended the call. "Those two really stick together."

Moss Stone knocked on the door to the home of Brooke Morgan. A minute passed and she opened the door, not looking pleased at Roberts and his arrival.

"I thought I told you everything at the police station."

"May we come in? I just have a couple more questions."

"Of course." She gave a tight-lipped smile.

After Stone sat in a living room chair, he flipped open his notebook. "You said you were with Paige Butler all night, the day Ryan died. Were there even a few minutes you weren't together?"

Brooke sat quietly for a few seconds. "I suppose for a few minutes when Paige went to the washroom. That would be it."

"Where was that?"

"At the coffee shop."

"Where was the coffee shop?"

Brooke frowned. "It was Charmain's Coffee Emporium."

"The one across the street from Ryan's office?"

"Yes, but that's ridiculous to think she would have a coffee with me, stop to run across the street, run back and finish her coffee and act like everything is normal."

"So, was she acting normal when she returned to the table?"

"She did act upset, but that was because her ex-girlfriend sent her a nasty text. That bothered her, obviously."

"Thank you for your help. We are trying to find who killed your husband, but so far, we haven't any strong leads. I trust you understand we're asking questions to help solve the murder, and not to just pester you with questions."

"Alright. Do you have any suspects?"

"No one in particular. We do have more information on the cause of Ryan's death, and that may help us as we assemble the clues together."

Stone and Roberts left, and they sat in Stone's car.

"Do you think Paige could dash from the coffee shop to Ryan's office, kill him, and return to the coffee shop within ten minutes?" Roberts asked.

"I think she could. Brooke did say she was acting upset when she returned to the table. But what about the money? Where would she put that?"

"Maybe she was the first one there of the two attacks. She stabbed him in the back and ran off, not considering he may still be alive. The second person arriving finishes him off and takes the money."

"Before we interview Paige again, let's check out the Joey's restaurant where she had dinner. Maybe the server, Suzz, will give us more information." Stone started his car. "Why don't you call to see if she's working tonight?"

"Sure, I can't imagine you making a phone call for an interview."

Stone started his car. As they pulled away from the curb, a Jeep hurried down the street. It parked in the driveway of Morgan's home.

"She made good time in arriving," Roberts commented as she listened to her phone.

"Yeah. It makes one wonder about their relationship. If they're that close, they would lie for one another. With Ryan out of the picture, they can spend more time together."

———

ROBERTS CONFIRMED THE SERVER WAS STARTING HER SHIFT AT 4:00 P.M.. Stone took his time driving to the south-side location. "Do you eat at Joeys?"

"Sometimes. Great food. The portions are small, which I like because then there's room for dessert."

Stone parked the car, and they made their way to the front entrance of the restaurant. He showed his police identification to the hostess, requesting to speak to Suzz. "She isn't in any trouble. We just want information on a customer she served," he explained when the hostess looked alarmed.

The hostess gave a quick smile and hurried away. Shortly later, she returned with a server following her.

"Hi, I'm Suzz. How can I help you?"

Stone used his phone to show a photo of Paige and Brooke. "Did you serve these women last Friday evening?"

"Yup. I think they were here around six, or a bit later."

"Okay, anything unusual happen? One woman said you'd remember them."

"No, nothing unusual. I remember them because the girl with the short hair flirted with me. She also left me a good tip. I think her name is Paige. She gave me her business card for some gym."

"Is that unusual?"

Suzz grinned. "No, flirting happens. What was different was a woman flirting with me. The other woman had a ring on her finger, so I wasn't sure of their relationship. In a way, they acted like they were on a date. Both were dressed up."

Stone thanked her and they returned to his car. "Well, at least we can confirm they were here. Also, that Paige and Brooke had a very close relationship."

"That doesn't mean they are killers."

"I suppose that's true. What troubles me is if Sutton is telling the truth, and that his knife wasn't used in the attack. Our coroner said there were two knives used. That likely means two people working together. If Paige and Brooke were not the killers, who is the next likely pair of collaborators?"

"Perhaps they were not any of our suspects. Possibly annoyed investors."

"There's nothing in his Day-Timer to indicate he had a meeting on Friday. Could it be other jealous girlfriends or annoyed husbands that got together for revenge?"

"That remains to be discovered. Want me to call Paige and arrange for a time to interview her again?"

"In the morning. I need to have dinner and think about the case."

———

PAIGE KNOCKED ON THE DOOR AND ENTERED. "ARE YOU ALRIGHT, Brooke?"

"Yes, I'm fine." Brooke walked across the living room and gave her a hug.

"What did the police want this time?"

"Just more questions." She went with Paige to the kitchen. "Wine?"

"Sure." She watched Brooke pour a red wine into a pair of glasses. The women sat at the kitchen counter on barstools.

"They asked me if at anytime on Friday you were not with me." Brooke took a sip of her wine. "I told them there were a few minutes we weren't together when you went to the washroom at the coffee shop."

"Oh." Paige swirled the wine in her glass.

"They asked if you acted different when you returned from the washroom." Brooke frowned. "I told them you had received a text from your ex, that it upset you."

"Okay. Did you tell them it was Charmain's?"

"Yes." She looked at the worried expression on Paige's face. "Did I say the wrong thing? I mean, I didn't want to lie to them. I know you weren't involved in Ryan's death."

"It's all good." She took a drink of the wine. "I just don't know why they keep asking us questions instead of finding the actual murderer."

"It's possible they believe we know more than we're saying."

"Brooke, that Detective Stone is like a dog with a bone. If he senses something is amiss, he keeps after it. I promise you, I had absolutely nothing to do with Ryan's death. But I do know something more."

"What is it?" Brooke took in a deep breath.

"Let me give Michael a call. It's best he's here when we talk about this."

"Is Michael involved in Ryan's murder? Please, tell me the truth."

"No. Michael had nothing to do with what happened to Ryan." She put down her wine glass and used her mobile to call Michael. After a quick conversation, she ended the call. "Michael is going to come over. I don't want to say anything more until he arrives."

"Alright, but this is making me anxious."

"Sorry. I know this is a tough time for you. But I'll be with you to get through this." She reached for Brooke's hand. "Michael wants to help too."

28

Tuesday Evening

BROOKE LOOKED AT PAIGE AND MICHAEL AS THEY STOOD IN HER LIVING room. "What's going on? This is about Ryan, isn't it?"

Paige looked at Michael.

He cleared his throat. "Brooke, this is really difficult for me to tell you this."

"Tell me what?"

"I went over to see Ryan Friday night. When I arrived, he was already dead. I panicked and ran away. I should've called the police, but I didn't. I made up a story I was in my apartment all night, but the detectives figured out I was lying." He took a deep breath. "I'm sorry I didn't tell you earlier."

Brooke crossed her arms. "Why did you lie to the police about being at Ryan's office?"

"Because I was going to see Ryan and do him harm. He was cheating on you, Brooke. He was stealing from Rover. Ryan had gone too far."

Paige joined in. "Ryan was blackmailing me with photos I had taken at university."

Brooke sat on the coach. "Why did you keep this from me?" She looked at Paige, then at Michael.

"I wasn't sure how to tell you Ryan was cheating on you. I wondered if you would think I was making it up, to make him look bad." Michael spread out his arms.

"Who was she?"

Michael held his hands together in front of him, holding his hands together. "Uh, there may have been more than one woman. Sorry, I know little more than that."

She looked back at Paige. "Did you know he was cheating on me?"

"I had strong suspicions. But I didn't know who."

Brooke started to cry. "You're my best friends and you didn't want to tell me this?"

"Brooke, you had to know he was cheating on you." Paige put her arm around her. "Did you really want us to tell you what you already knew?"

"I guess not." She wiped away her tears. "What were you going to do to Ryan? You said harming him? Does that mean killing him?"

"I honestly don't know. I was going to smack him around, tell him he had to treat you and everyone better. To be honest, I was going to do whatever it took to prevent him from hurting you."

"I'll refill your wine glass." Paige took her empty glass and went to the kitchen.

Brooke stared at Michael. "I'm not sure how I feel about you. Going to Ryan's office to do him harm? You know I hate violence. Doing that to help me makes that even worse."

———

PAIGE WENT TO THE KITCHEN, OPENING A DOOR WHERE LIQUOR WAS KEPT. She made a straight rum for Michael and refilled the two wine glasses. When she returned to the living room, Michael was on the coach, holding a crying Brooke. "How are you feeling?"

Brooke sighed. "Angry, sad, upset, and a bunch of other things. I also feel relief that I don't have to put up with Ryan's dealings and affairs anymore. That makes me feel guilty."

Paige took her by her hand. "Come, let's sit outside. The fresh air will help us feel better."

———

MICHAEL FOLLOWED THE TWO WOMEN OUTSIDE, HOPING HE DIDN'T HAVE to give any more details about Friday night. *I don't enjoy evading the truth.* He sat in one of the chairs around the small patio tables, equally spaced between Brooke and Paige, forming a triangle.

29

August 29, Wednesday Morning

DETECTIVE MOSS STONE WALKED UP THE SHORT SIDEWALK TO THE HALF-duplex home. "It appears Paige Butler has a more modest income than our other suspects."

"That's true. But Ryan Morgan had the most money and looked at what happened to him."

"Good point." He pushed the doorbell.

The door opened. Paige stood wearing black, tight -fitting shorts and a white crop top. "Come on in. I've made coffee."

"Thank you." Roberts entered first, sitting in one of the two unmatched armchairs.

Stone looked around the small living room and sat in the other armchair.

Paige called out from the kitchen. "What do you take in your coffee?"

"Just milk."

"Black."

A minute later, Paige entered, carrying three mugs. She gave Roberts her coffee first and handed over a mug to Stone. "I'll bet my coffee is better than your tea."

"I wouldn't doubt it." He waited until she sat on the remaining place to sit, a loveseat, then asked, "We were reviewing your statements about the Friday night when Ryan Morgan died. I understand you stated you were with Brooke Morgan during the evening. However, there turns out a period in Charmaine's Coffee Emporium where you were not with her. You went or said you went, to the washroom. During that time, you had the opportunity to hurry across the street to Ryan's office, kill him, and return to the coffee shop."

Paige gave a half smile. "You know I went out for dinner that evening, don't you?"

Stone nodded. "We do."

"Have you considered what I was wearing?"

"No, what difference does that make?"

"You can check with Brooke or the server at Joey's. Or at the coffee shop. I was wearing a short, tight black skirt with high heels. It's not something I would dash across the street in and attack a man in. I think you may have me confused with one of Charlie's Angels." She looked at Roberts. "Tell your detective partner what it's like wearing heels and trying to do anything fast."

Roberts sighed. "She has a point. Unless you're watching a movie, you won't see a woman fight, or run, in heels."

"Damn." He took a drink of his coffee. "Okay, I get it." He peered at Paige. "I'm curious. Do you carry a knife with you? In a purse?"

Paige frowned. "A purse? Me carrying a purse big enough to hide a knife? I don't think so. But I have a knife. It's in the glove compartment in my Jeep. Want me to get it?"

"Under the circumstances, it may be best if I get it. Where are the keys?"

Paige shrugged, stood, and walked to the kitchen, returning with a set of keys. She placed them in his hand. "Make sure you lock the Jeep afterward."

"Will do." Stone walked to the kitchen, exiting out the rear door.

"More coffee?" Paige asked Roberts.

"Sure. You don't seem nervous about the knife."

"No reason to be. I didn't kill Ryan, and I've never used that knife. I bought it for protection and never had a reason to use it. Yet." She refilled the cups.

"Do you have an opinion about who killed Ryan?"

"No. Just that it's hard to believe anyone I know would have done it."

"How about Michael? He was carrying a knife when he went to see Ryan. That sounds like an intent to murder."

"He may have been carrying a knife, but I find it hard to believe he would have used it."

"Why?"

"Michael..., he knows restraint. He could be furious, or upset, but he always stops from going over the edge. He may have had the knife, but I don't believe he would've used it."

"Okay. Would you have?"

Paige smiled. "No. I could have handled Ryan without a knife."

"Did you consider teaching him a lesson when he showed you the photos of yourself?"

"No. I was just pissed off. What did you think of the photos?"

"They were nice. I guess for nudes, they were in good taste."

"Do you think you can get a copy of them and send them to me? I never got a copy of the photos."

"I'll see what I can do."

"Thanks. If you ever want lessons on self-defence, I would be glad to provide some to you."

"I'll keep that in mind. For now, I'm good."

Stone entered the room, holding a knife in a plastic bag. "There doesn't appear to be any signs of blood on it, but our lab will take a closer look."

"There won't be. Just make sure you return it afterward."

Roberts followed Stone out the door and toward his car. "Did you find anything besides the knife?"

"No. Clean vehicle. Did you learn anything more from her?"

"She's convinced Michael wouldn't have murdered Ryan Morgan, even if he was alive when he arrived at his office. She doesn't know who might have murdered him."

"The knife looks brand new. No marks on it. I'm not optimistic our lab will find anything on it."

"By the way, Paige wants a copy of her photos."

"Makes sense. She seems fairly confident about her body."

"What's our next step? Who do you want to focus on?"

"Good question." He started his car. "I want to interview the secretary of the year again, and I want to look around Joseph McCarthy's home for something."

"What is that something?"

"I'm not sure. I don't believe his alibi."

"Okay, so which one should we work on? Melisa or Joseph?"

"I'm not sure." He tapped the steering wheel with his fingers. He looked out the driver's window.

"What are you looking at?"

"A hint from the universe what to do next."

"Seriously?" She looked at the mix of duplexes and single-family homes. Nothing appeared out of the ordinary, and she was about to say so when she spotted a man working on a roof to adjust a satellite dish. "There's a man on a roof. Other than that, I see nothing."

"The roof? Okay, I know who to see next."

"Who?"

"Rover Driscoll. He works on roofs. Let's interview him again."

Roberts shook her head. "Your logic really is something else."

30

Wednesday Afternoon

ROBERTS CALLED ROVER DRISCOLL, LEARNING WHERE HE WAS WORKING. They drove to the west end of the city, seeing three men working on a roof of a bungalow. On the front lawn, a dark-skinned man was loading bundles of asphalt tiles onto a conveyor belt. The conveyor belt dropped the bundles onto the roof, where the other workers distributed the tiles.

Stone parked his car and strolled to the man loading the asphalt tiles. He didn't see Rover or his truck. Stone waved at the man to draw his attention.

"Excuse me, we're looking for Rover Driscoll. Is he around here?" He spoke over the rumbling of the conveyor belt. Stone showed his police identification.

"Rover? No, he went to pick up more water. He'll be back soon." He eyed the police badge suspiciously.

"Have you worked for Rover long?"

"A few months."

Stone saw the tattoos on his arms and made an assumption. "Are you part of the church's second chance program?"

"Yes, I am."

"Okay, last Friday, were you working with Rover?"

"Yes, sir."

"Late afternoon, until five pm. Was he with you?"

"He was. We were at a different site and worked until seven."

"Anything unusual happen? Did he disappear for a bit? Like to get water?"

"No. He was with us."

"Did he ask you to do him a favour? Something illegal, perhaps?"

The man licked his lips and looked around. Up on the roof, the other men were watching. "Look, it was no big deal. Rover asked me if I could run a bobcat on some property next to the church to level it out. It wasn't entirely legal, 'cause it wasn't the church's property. But it was just an unused field that was a hazard, so we cleaned it up on Saturday."

Stone saw Rover's truck pull up. The big man quickly approached Stone and Roberts.

"What's going on here? Dermot, you don't have to talk to them if you don't want to."

Stone held up his hand. "Relax, we were just waiting for you. Dermot just informed us you were at the work site on Friday."

"Alright. I just don't want the cops to harass my guys, that's all."

"Mr. Driscoll, we're investigating the murder of your friend, Ryan Morgan. If we're asking questions, I can guarantee it isn't to harass anyone. Unless you've got something to hide, I expect your full cooperation. If you have a beef with the police, keep it to yourself."

Rover's snarl disappeared. "You're right. The Lord would not approve of me holding a grudge against the police. I apologize."

"Alright." Stone was surprised at his sudden change in attitude. "Do you know of anyone else who may have had hard feelings with Ryan Morgan? Another investor? Someone he may have had an affair with?"

"No. The truth is I invested in Ryan's business not because of a potential return on my investment, but because he was an acquaintance of Lydia's. I wanted to establish a friendship with as many people as I could with the people she knew. I left my old life behind and needed to establish a different circle of acquaintances."

"But your feelings for Ryan changed later."

"It did." Rover sighed. "I saw the man was a liar, a cheater and a fraud. I could live with a poor investment return because money is not an issue with me, but it appeared I might lose it all if Ryan declared the bar bankrupt. Plus, the fact his character didn't stand up to scrutiny. I visited him in his office and gave fair warning I expected better results, and he assured me things were back to normal. I left it at that. To answer your earlier questions, I didn't know of any other investors or of anyone he was having an affair with."

"Alright. Do you know who this is?" Stone held up his phone, showing a head shot of a blonde woman.

"Yes." He thought for a moment. "Her name is Jill and she works at the Hi-Lite Bar."

"You were at a bar?"

"Yes, to check it out." He frowned. "That's the bar I invested money in through Ryan. In case you're wondering, I only had a pop to drink."

"I wasn't wondering, but good for you to know what you need to do to avoid problems."

"Thanks, I appreciate that. I know I have to be careful. The devil is watching me, waiting for me to make a mistake."

Stone and Roberts left, getting into his vehicle. Stone commented, "If the devil is watching us to make a mistake, he must have his hands full with you."

"Me? You're one to talk."

Stone laughed. "Man, you're easy to tease."

Roberts glared at him. "So now what do we do?"

"Let's visit the McCarthys."

––––––––

RACHEL MCCARTHY OPENED THE DOOR, HER FACE SHOWING SURPRISE AS she peered at Stone and Roberts. "That was fast. You just called."

"We were in the neighbourhood," Stone replied.

"Come in. I'll tell Joe you're here."

Stone entered the living room with Roberts. He watched Rachael stand at the open doorway and call out to the basement. Moments later, a thumping on the staircase indicated Joseph McCarthy was making his way up.

Stone remained standing, eyeing Joseph. "Mr. McCarthy, we're here just to clear up a few details. Do you mind if I look around as I ask a few questions?"

"No, not at all." Joseph cast a look at Rachael. "Is there something specific you want to look at?"

"No. Maybe a case of I'll know it when I see it."

Stone strolled into the modern-designed kitchen. He looked at the windows with the cloth curtains and turned his attention to the clean marble counters. A black plated toaster, a mixer and a coffee machine sat on the hard surface below the cupboards. Next to the black toaster stood a wood block holding a half-dozen knives. He pulled out a knife, examining the eight-inch knife.

"What are you looking at?"

"Just curious. This is the length of knife used to kill Ryan Morgan."

"I assure you, it has never left the kitchen. And if it was used to kill someone, I doubt we would put it back in the block for dinner preparation."

"A valid point." Stone continued his search around the kitchen, opening cupboards and drawers. He saw Joseph had crossed his arms as he watched him. "Can we look downstairs?"

"Sure." Joseph slowly nodded. "It's this way."

Stone followed him out of the kitchen and past a doorway that led to the downstairs.

The basement looked neat, with storage shelves on the far end of the wall. On another wall was a workbench, and next to it was a table with wood carving tools and partially finished wooden horse. Lights were positioned over the workbench and the table.

Stone saw the laminate floor was clean and walked to the workbench. All the tools were put away. A metal tool case sat on the workbench, and he opened a few of the drawers, finding pliers, drill bits and other tools organized separately in the different compartments. A set of screwdrivers sat in a holder. All of them were organized according to style and size. He turned his attention to the table.

It was clean, with the carving knives placed in a box next to the horse he was working on. "I see the box contains six knives, but there is an empty spot for a seventh knife. Where is that knife?"

"It doesn't exist. I bought the other knives second hand. It didn't have the largest knife included." He gave a short smile. "I guess that's why it was so cheap."

"You didn't buy a replacement knife?"

"No. I'm planning to once I become more familiar with wood carving. Then I'll know which knife, or knives, to buy."

"So you made this horse without all the proper knives?" He picked up the horse, turning it over in his hands. "It looks pretty good."

"Thanks. I'm still learning how to make the cuts."

Stone put down the wood carving, noticing two paperback books on wood carving. He picked one up and opened it near the beginning. In bold letters, the book emphasised it was important to have the proper tools to start with. Trying to carve, it stated, without the correct knife would doom the project. Stone put down the book and turned to see Joseph staring at him.

———

WHILE STONE WENT ABOUT THE HOUSE LOOKING AROUND, ROBERTS SAT IN the living room with Rachael.

"What does Joseph know about your affair and the photographs?"

Rachael looked at the floor before speaking to Roberts. Her face turned pink. "I told him of the affair, and that there were pictures taken."

"Did he see the photos?"

"No. I haven't seen them either. I wish they would disappear. It's so embarrassing and I'm ashamed I did it."

"Does Joseph know it was Ryan who you were having an affair with?"

She shook her head. "No, I told him it was someone he didn't know. I'm grateful Joe forgave me."

"We have all done things we regret."

"Thank you for your understanding, but this is a truly big mistake."

"On the Friday Ryan was killed, you said you were home while Joseph went to the gym."

"That's right."

"Was anyone with you? What did you do?"

"I spent the time taking a bath and getting myself ready. Joe and I are making amends with each other, me more than him, and I wanted to look my best."

"After Joe returned from the gym, how did he act? Happy, nervous, excited?"

"I suppose a bit excited or a tad nervous." She smiled. "Joe isn't much for horror movies. I think he wasn't too keen on seeing the movie, but he was willing to go to make me happy."

"It sounds like he would do anything for you."

"Yes, he's a good man. I wish I had never cheated on him. I was so selfish."

"The important thing is you're back together."

"I suppose that's true."

"He must have been upset with Ryan if he found out it was him."

Rachael hesitated before answering. "I guess he would be, but Joe doesn't get emotional about things. To be honest, it relieved him when I told him I wanted to work things out with him. You may think Joe would seek revenge on whoever I had an affair with, but Joe isn't a violent man. I can't believe he would attack anyone."

"Sometimes people react differently than we expect under unusual circumstances."

"I suppose. But not Joe. He's quite predicable. When he stopped reading the newspaper all evening, that was a major change. He would never become a murderer. That's simply not who he is."

Roberts heard and then saw Stone and Joseph had returned upstairs. She stood.

"We're about done here," Stone announced. He followed Roberts out the front door as the McCarthys stood at the doorway, watching them leave.

When Stone closed the driver's door, he turned to Roberts. "What did you get out of your interview?"

"That her husband isn't capable of violence, that he just doesn't overreact to situations. I have to agree Joe doesn't seem the type to commit murder. He appears rather reserved. She also claims Joe didn't know it was Ryan she had an affair with. What did you find out?"

"Clean and tidy kitchen and workshop. Tools all orderly. Worktable was also clean. There were a couple of books on woodcarving. He had a set of carving knives. He was missing one knife, and he claimed he bought as a used set, and it was missing one knife."

"Do you believe that?"

"I do. I also believe he knew Ryan was the one having an affair with his wife, and he's guilty of stabbing Ryan Morgan."

"He has an alibi. He was at the gym at the time."

"He does claim that. I think we should pay a visit to the gym."

"Now?"

"No, let's do it the morning. I think we've done enough for one day. I'll see you in the office tomorrow."

31

Thursday Morning

Stone parked his car at Fit-Right Gym, looking around at nearby vehicles. The gym had a large parking lot, having taken over the location from a grocery store. "It looks like they're doing a good business of getting people to exercise."

"Diet and exercise are an obsession for some people." Roberts closed her car door.

"I prefer beer and bikes." He opened the door to the gym and Roberts entered the brightly lit interior.

Stone approached the front counter. To the left side was a gate. A man approached the gate and used a plastic card on a card reader to unlock the door.

A smiling woman behind the counter greeted them. "Are you first-time visitors? We have a special discount for couples." A name tag showed her name was Stephanie.

Stone showed his police badge. "We're here on a different sort of exercise." He showed a picture of Joseph McCarthy on his phone. "Do you recognize him? He said he was here last Friday."

The woman studied the photo. "He looks familiar, but I can't say for certain he was here on Friday. What's his name? I can check the log entry."

Stone told her his name and watched as she typed an entry on a keyboard.

"Yes, his card was used on Friday. The time was four-seventeen in the afternoon."

"Could someone else have used his card?"

"Not likely. His photograph is on the card and Nicole watches the guests as they enter. We take turns covering the entrance." She pointed at a petite brunette at the end of the counter. "I can ask her if she saw him on Friday."

"Please do."

Nicole walked over to where Stone and Roberts stood when Stephanie called her over.

"How can I help you?"

Stone showed the photo again. "Do you recall seeing him last Friday?"

"Yes, he was very friendly. Gave me a wave as he entered."

"Okay. Mr. McCarthy also said he talked to a Tom Kassian, a trainer here."

"Sure, he's here right now. I'll get him." Stephanie disappeared into an office behind the counter. A few moments later, a tall, athletic man appeared.

"How can I help you?"

"Do you recall talking to this man?"

"Sure. He asked about the cost of a personal trainer. I think it was a few days ago."

"Do you recall the time you spoke with him?"

He closed his eyes, then opened them. "Yes, it was shortly before I was going to get something to eat. It was a bit after five pm, or closer to half-past five." He looked pleased at his memory recall.

Stone thanked him and noticed the exit doors were set away from the entrance area. He commented to Roberts. "They don't check to see who's leaving."

"Are you thinking Joseph could have left immediately after checking in, drove to Morgan's office, murdered him, and then returned here?"

"It is possible. Morgan's office is a twenty to twenty-five minute drive. He could have murdered our victim and returned here in time to have a conversation with the personal trainer to establish his alibi that he was here at the time. And..." Stone pointed at the entrance, "some people are entering without a card. Nicole is buzzing them through."

"Let's ask if it's possible Joseph was able to enter a second time that way." Roberts walked to counter and beckoned Nicole to speak with her.

"We noticed some people were allowed to enter without a card. Can you tell us about those circumstances?"

"Sure. Some are here to see our massage therapist, and they wouldn't necessarily have a membership for that. The other situation is if a member forgot his card, or if a person was on a trial membership or visitor's pass."

"Okay, thanks." Roberts looked at Stone, who was staring at the entrance. "What do you see?"

"Two members entered. The first used his card to open the gate. The second member stopped the gate from closing. He did touch his card at the card reader, so it likely acknowledged he arrived as well. But what if Joseph, when he returned a second time, followed a member in without using his card?"

"You mean he pretended to use his card in case someone was watching, but never registered his second visit?"

"Exactly. That leads to the problem of proving that's what he did. It also makes me wonder who used the second knife to slice Morgan's throat. I'm thinking our mild-mannered Joseph had a cohort he met to deal with our victim." Stone began to walk to the exit.

Roberts followed him. "His wife?"

"Perhaps. But I don't get that vibe from her. Like, she is a petite woman who doesn't strike me as someone that would wield a knife. I'm thinking more along the line of one of his buddies. For example, Michael or Rover."

"Rover has a pretty good alibi." She opened the car door.

"True. But we do know Michael was there. Perhaps he didn't just discover the body but was the killer along with Joseph."

"Okay, if we go with that, then Joseph's wood carving knife was used to stab Ryan Morgan in the back. That may be appropriate, seeing he was having an affair with Rachael. Joseph would have felt betrayed by his golfing buddy. But where is the second knife? The large knife we found in the dumpster hadn't been used."

"Yeah, there is that problem as well." He started the car. "Maybe the second person was Paige Butler. Maybe she did jog over to help out Joseph from the coffee shop."

"But where is the knife she would have used?"

"I don't know. But let's go to that coffee shop and see if the other employees saw her leave for a few minutes."

"Louise said Andrews was attending tables at the time. Let's check if he's available now."

————

STONE AND ROBERTS STEPPED OUT OF THE PARKED CAR IN FRONT OF Charmaine's Coffee Emporium. They entered the coffee shop and went to the front counter and waited until the manager, Louise, finished with a pair of customers.

"Hi, you need more information?" Louise asked after she walked to where they waited.

"Yes," Stone replied. "You mentioned Andrew worked the tables and may have noticed more about the customers."

"Yes, and he's here right now." She pointed at a young man cleaning a table.

"Thanks." Stone went over to the medium built, sandy-coloured hair man.

"Excuse me, can we ask you a couple of questions?" Stone showed him his identification.

Andrew suddenly looked nervous.

"It has nothing to do with you, just a couple of customers you may have served," Stone explained.

"Oh, sure." He looked relieved.

Roberts held up her mobile. "Do you recognize this woman from Friday afternoon?" She showed an image of Paige Butler.

"Oh, yeah, sure. I remember her. She was with another woman. A blonde."

Roberts showed him another photo, this one of Brooke Morgan. "Was this the other woman?"

"Yes, that was her."

"Do you recall if during their coffee together, did one of them leave the coffee shop for a few minutes?" Roberts looked through the windows, seeing the street and the building where Ryan Morgan had his office.

"No, I don't think so. But the first lady did go to the washroom and afterward was just standing there and watching something through the windows. I looked to see what she was watching but didn't see anything."

"She just watched, didn't go outside?"

Andrew shook his head. "No, she just went to her table afterward."

Roberts showed him another photograph, this one of the servers identified as Jill by Rover. "Have you seen her here?"

"No, I don't remember seeing her before."

"Okay, how about her?" Roberts showed a photo of Melisa.

"Hmm, yes, she was here. She was here earlier on Friday. She had a table by the window."

"Was she alone?"

"She was at first. Then some guy sat at her table."

"What did he look like?" Roberts noticed Stone was scribbling notes as he listened to her questions. "Can you describe him?"

"No, not really. White guy, dark hair. That's about all I remember."

"How tall was he?" Roberts persisted with her questioning.

Andrew shrugged. "Average, I guess. Taller than she was."

"What was he wearing?"

"I don't know. Nothing special. Jeans and a t-shirt. Sorry, I wasn't paying any attention to him."

"But you can describe her?"

"Sure. Short blue skirt, high heels, nice hair."

"How long did they stay?" Stone asked.

"Not long. He didn't even have a coffee. She didn't finish hers."

"Did you see where they went afterward?"

"No, I just cleaned off their table."

Stone sighed. "Okay, thanks for your help."

After Andrew left, Roberts asked, "What do think of that interview?"

"I think Andrew has a real strong eye for the ladies. Men, not so much. I also would really like to ask our office-manager girl what she was doing here about the time of Ryan Morgan's murder."

"I'll phone to see if she's at home and not having her nails done."

———

STONE STEPPED TOWARD THE APARTMENT TOWER ENTRANCE AND HELD THE door open for Roberts. "I'm wondering who the man was she was meeting. Someone involved in the murder?"

"That would mean it also involved Melisa in the murder."

"Yeah, maybe she isn't all peaches and cream."

They reached the elevator and rode it to the floor. Melisa quickly opened the door to their knock.

"Detective Stone, it's nice to see you again. Please come in."

Stone walked toward the kitchen, looking at the stainless-steel appliances. Next to the kitchen, glass shelves displayed a few bottles of spirits. A wine rack hung on the wall nearby, showing off a half-dozen bottles of wine.

"Nicely stocked bar."

"Thank you. I only drink wine, but I keep other liquor for guests."

Stone joined Roberts and sat on the couch, facing Melisa sitting across from them.

"Ms. Regan, according to a witness, you were at Charmain's Coffee

Emporium on the Friday Ryan Morgan died." Stone looked at her, waiting for her to reply.

"Yes, I suppose I was. I sometimes go there after work."

"Can you tell us the reason you were there?"

"It's a coffee shop. I went there for a coffee." Sarcasm dripped from her voice.

"So, you went for a coffee and sat by yourself? Did you do anything while sitting there?"

"I drank my coffee." She sighed.

"Did you talk to anyone?"

Melisa eyed Stone suspiciously. "Why do you ask? I'm not opposed to be talking to people. Often men come up to me and ask for my name and number."

"You're being evasive." Stone raised his voice at her. "You met someone at Charmaine's. Who was it and why?"

"I don't like your tone, Detective Stone." Melisa glared at him. "Yes, I met someone at the coffee shop. He contacted me and wanted a date. I met him there and turned him down. Do I have to explain to you what a date means?"

"You're an escort. A date in your business is pretty self-explanatory. What was his name? Why did you turn him down?"

"I can't remember his name. I turned him down because I didn't have a good feeling about him. That's one of the reasons I met him in the coffee shop. I didn't want him to know where I lived. I usually have a few dates first before I let someone to my apartment."

"Alright. You just turned him down, and he left. He wasn't upset?" Stone scribbled in his notebook.

"No. I told him the price of my company. It was too high for him. I was glad he just walked away."

"Okay. Can you tell me what he looked like and what he was wearing?"

"I don't remember. He didn't leave an impression on me. I guess average looking. That's all."

"Was he white, coloured? Dark hair? What kind of shirt was he wearing?"

"White. I don't know what shirt he was wearing or the colour of his hair. Like I said, he didn't leave an impression on me. I forgot him as soon as he left."

Stone checked his notes. "Do you have anything to add to your coffee meeting?"

"No. Quite frankly, you're wasting my time with these questions."

Stone glanced at Roberts, who looked toward the ceiling. "Very well, that's all the questions for now. You may regret not being more forthcoming."

"I'm telling you all I know."

Stone closed his notebook. "I don't believe you." He stood. "We'll be in contact with you again."

Stone and Roberts left the apartment, with Melisa slamming the door behind them.

"I don't believe she wants to be your friend anymore," Roberts commented.

"The feeling is mutual."

"You told her you thought she was lying."

"She is." He entered the elevator. "There's no way she didn't remember what a potential client looked like if she rejected him from his appearance or lack of funds. Second, our witness, Andrew, said she left with him. The guy, whoever he was, wore jeans and a t-shirt. Tell me, if he was a client who could be wanting to make use of her services, why would he be wearing jeans? A suit would be closer to the attire for a man able to make use of her company."

"Good points." She looked at him as the car came to a halt. "Is this mystery man her accomplice in Ryan's murder?"

"He could be. Who do we know that wears casual clothes and would conspire with her to murder Ryan Morgan?"

"Rover?"

"Yes and no." Stone walked from the elevator to the front doors of the apartment. "He wears casual clothes, but he has a good alibi. Besides, I think Andrew would remember a big guy like that."

They walked toward his car. "Where to next?" Roberts asked.

"The Hi-Lite Bar. I want to talk to that server, Jill Campbell."

———

ROBERTS FOLLOWED STONE INTO THE BAR. HER EYES ADJUSTED TO THE lower lights, and she glanced around the interior. The pub was clean, with the tables and chairs organized in a pattern. The best light was where the bar was set up, with the beer taps at the front and bottles of spirits displayed on a glass shelf at the back. While there wasn't one thing that bothered her, the overall impression was that it was a place she would avoid going to on a night out with her friends. She saw Stone was approaching a tall man, who appeared to be the manager.

Stone held up his police identification. "Are you in charge here?"

"Yup, at least until the new owners take over."

"What's your name?" Stone flipped open his notebook.

"Mitch Harold." He crossed his arms. "Can you tell me what the hell is going on? I heard the owner was murdered, and I'm not sure that I'm supposed to even have the bar open, let alone if I continue to order supplies."

"Sorry, I can't help you there. Did you know the owner?"

"We met a few times."

"What did you think of him?"

Mitch frowned. "I didn't like him. Acted like a big shot."

"Were you surprised he was killed?"

"No, can't say I was. Look, he had a shady side to him. He allowed a drug gang to use this bar to make transactions in return for a cut of the pie. It's scared off a few customers and I don't ask the girls to serve their tables. That I handle myself. No point at putting them at risk. But I'm telling you, I was looking for a new place to work before he was killed."

"Was there a lot of money involved in these drug dealings?"

"It was more than what the bar made legitimately. Look, I have work to do. My cook didn't show up for his shift, so I gotta cover that."

"The cook didn't show up? What's his name?"

"Tyler." He stopped and thought a moment. "Tyler Harris. He's been a no show before. He has a drug problem and gets too wasted to make it in some days. I'd can him, but it's hard to find help these days. He's actually a pretty smart dude, good cook. He just has an addiction problem."

"Was he here last Friday?"

"He worked the weekend shifts. From about six to closing. He had Monday and Tuesday off."

"Was he here yesterday?"

"He was. Look, it's not unusual for Tyler to go on a bender. He's missed a few days now and then."

"Okay. We're looking for a Jill Campbell. Is she on shift today?"

"Yup." He pointed to where a blonde was cleaning up around the VLT machines. "That be her."

"Thanks. Could you get me Tyler's phone and address? We may want to talk to him."

"Sure, give me a minute." Mitch turned and walked to the back of the bar.

"Anya, why don't you have a conversation with the server? I'll wait for Mitch."

"Sure." Roberts walked to the back of the bar, approaching the waitress. "Hi, can I ask you a few questions?" She held up her identification.

Jill nodded and stopped wiping down the VLT machines. "Is this about Ryan Morgan?"

"Yes. How well did you know him?"

"Not too well. He came in here a couple of times. It was mostly to talk to Mitch."

"We found photos of you on his computer." Roberts watched her reaction.

"Oh, shit. Can you delete those? I shouldn't have posed for them. I went to his office with a girlfriend, you know, as protection, and he gave me a couple of hundred bucks to let him take photos. I'm glad my girlfriend was with me, 'cause I was feeling really uncomfortable later. He was leering at me as he took the pictures."

"What did Mitch and Ryan talk about?"

"I don't know, but he told off Mitch one time. I don't think they liked each other."

"What do you know about Tyler Harris?"

"He's okay. Takes drugs. This isn't a place he should be working. Too much drugs in this place."

"Anything else you know about Ryan Morgan?"

"No." She shook her head. "But can you get rid of those pictures? I don't want anyone else to see them."

"I'll do what I can." Roberts walked back to where Stone was standing.

"Find anything useful, Anya?"

"No, other than more confirmation, our victim was one sleezy character. According to Jill, he didn't have a good relationship with Mitch. I guess that is to be expected."

"I showed a photo of Melisa Regan to him, but he didn't recognize her." Stone walked toward the exit. "I think there's a lot of illegal stuff happening here, but possibly not related to our murder."

"I agree, but is it just a coincidence Tyler Harris is missing from work so soon after Morgan was murdered?"

"Good question. I have his phone number and address. Let's see if we can dig out more information on him."

They walked to his car while Roberts made the phone call. After listening a few moments, she announced there wasn't an answer. "It just went to voice mail. I didn't leave a message."

"Damn. This case is frustrating. Everyone has an alibi or isn't available for questioning."

"Well, you can't expect criminals to want to make it easy to be caught."

"I suppose. But most criminals aren't that smart." He started his car. "But if you look at the people Ryan Morgan associated with, most of them are university educated. So I guess we may be dealing with smart criminals."

Roberts did up her seat belt. "That may make it more interesting. Do you have a primary suspect?"

"No, just the knowledge suspects have been lying to us. Joseph McCarthy is lying about his missing wood carving knife. I believe Rachael McCarthy told him who she was having the affair with. But if

Joseph did stab Morgan in the back, then who finished him with another knife? Melisa is also lying to us, but is she a person who would attack our victim with a knife? I have trouble picturing her wielding a knife."

"Don't underestimate her. Long nails or not, I'll bet she can use a knife to get what she wants."

"I learned a long time ago not to underestimate women."

"Because we're smarter?"

"No, more devious. I think it's time to pay a visit to Joseph McCarthy. I want to see if we can shake him up a bit. He's hiding information from us."

32

Late Thursday Afternoon

STONE AND ROBERTS ARRIVED AT THE McCARTHY HOME. A FEW MINUTES later, Rachel McCarthy greeted them.

Stone sat on the couch next to Roberts. "We have a few questions we would like to clear up." Stone looked at Joseph and Rachael, took a drink of his coffee, and opened his notebook. "I am impressed by how well you made up your alibi, Joseph. Details planned out. You even got your wife to lie about your knowledge of Ryan having an affair with Rachael." He watched as they exchanged glances.

"Rachael told me a couple of days ago. I was shocked at the time, but that's water under the bridge now." Joseph grabbed his coffee cup, perspiration appeared on his forehead.

"Mr. McCarthy, you look a bit distraught there." Stone paused and looked at his notes. "Do you know the cause of death of Ryan Morgan?"

"Huh? I understand he was stabbed. I assumed so because you asked about my knives." Joseph placed down his coffee cup.

"He was. In the back. Three times. Whoever stabbed him in the back

172

left him to die."

"That, that's terrible."

"Yeah, it was. Except here's another detail." Stone watched Joseph's face. "Whoever stabbed him in the back didn't kill him. Ryan Morgan was alive when you left him, Joseph. He was crawling to his desk when a second visitor arrived. Mr. McCarthy, you didn't murder Ryan Morgan." He watched as Joseph's jaw dropped and his shoulders sagged. "Do you want to confess to attempted murder now?"

Joseph shook his head. "I, I thought..."

Rachel grabbed his arm. "Don't say anything."

"He doesn't have to. I can see the truth in his face. I may not prove he stabbed Ryan right now, but I know he did it."

Joseph closed his eyes. "How did Ryan die?"

"That's still on a need-to-know basis. I will tell you that if you had arrived ten minutes after you did, you may have been murdered as well. Something for you to think about. In the meantime, as the saying goes, don't leave town. I still want to prove you attacked Ryan Morgan and attempted to murder him." Stone stood. "I'll leave you with an option. Confess you attacked him, and I'll have the charge reduced from attempted murder to assault causing bodily harm." He stared at the shaken man. "Let me know sooner than later."

Stone left with Roberts. Before they reached his car, Roberts asked, "Do you think he'll confess?"

"No, I don't. But he now knows I know, and that should make him wonder if I can prove it. Maybe a few more restless nights' sleep."

"Fair enough. What do you want to do next?"

"Let's return to the scene of the crime. We might find a few more clues to help us."

———

"WHAT DO YOU HOPE TO DISCOVER HERE? I THOUGHT YOU HAD CHECKED out his office already." Anya Roberts looked around Ryan Morgan's office, pivoting around in a circle to face Stone.

"We had a murder. Here. The murderer, or perhaps murderers, was in this office. In quantum mechanics, any interference, even observation from the outside changes a closed system. I'm going to find what the murderers changed here. Maybe that will help reveal their identity."

Stone moved around the office, wearing gloves. He examined the outline of Ryan's body, opening and closing desk drawers, looked inside the empty safe, and checked the inside of the closet. He picked up a partial bottle of Tennessee whiskey from the top of a credenza. "This is the one thing in the office that does not belong here."

"Do you think it belongs to the killer?" She studied the bottle. "Maybe it's something our victim keeps in the office to have a drink now and then."

"Ryan Morgan was a high-roller. I don't believe this whiskey would be his style. Maybe eighteen-year-old Scotch Whisky, or Maker's Mark Bourbon, but he wouldn't have anything not on a top shelf in a liquor store for himself."

"Yet we have this bottle."

"Yeah, there is that. Perhaps someone else brought it here." He left the inner office and walked into the main office, paused, and sat at Melisa Regan's desk. Stone opened and closed the drawers, not finding anything interesting. He stood and went to the rear of the office, where the coffee machine sat on a counter. He briefly looked at the selection of the capsules in a metal stand and checked the underneath the counter. Stone frowned at the napkins, supplies of sugar and powdered milk substitute.

A small fridge underneath the counter didn't provide any more information for him, and he opened a dishwasher.

"Hmm." He slid out the top drawer, revealing coffee cups and three tumblers. He picked each one in turn and sniffed the cup. "Jack Daniels. Two with lipstick smudges on them."

"So Ryan had a small party here with two women? Maybe one of them was Melisa Regan." Roberts stood at the doorway to the coffee room.

"No, Melisa, the office manager, told us she drinks only wine. I suspect the two women were Jill and her girlfriend. Ryan likely took the photos here."

"From my experience, men rarely put anything in the dishwasher. I'll bet Melisa was the one putting the glasses away the following morning."

"If that's the case, she wouldn't be too pleased with Ryan for having a party without her. He was cheating on his wife to hang around with her, and maybe it didn't go too well to learn he was also cheating on her."

"Good grief. He was married, making out with Melisa, having an affair with Rachael McCarthy, and chasing after Jill. He's a regular Don Juan. A sleezy Don Juan."

"How did he find time for work and sleep?" Stone asked. He walked to Melisa's desk and sat facing the computer monitor. He hit the enter key on the keyboard. In the centre of the screen, a password was requested. He stared at the screen.

"We can take the computer in and have one of our techs unlock the password." Roberts stood behind his shoulder.

"Or, we can find it ourselves." He flipped over the keyboard. On the base, a sticky note had the word 'ParisInSpring'. He typed in the password, and the screen revealed various folders. He opened them, one by one, seeing the usual letters of correspondence, spreadsheets, invoices, and other documents. A spreadsheet listed the employees of Hi-Lite Bar, including phone numbers and addresses. "Nothing of much interest here." Stone opened the internet browser, going to the settings and checking the history. "She sure checks her social media accounts a lot."

"Some people do that. Nothing unusual there." Roberts shrugged.

"Hey, maybe there's something here." He clicked on the icon of the recycle bin, listing the deleted files. He restored several documents, quickly scanning their contents. A Word document caused him to say, "Aha!"

"It seems she was offering a hefty monetary reward to Tyler for his help." Roberts read the brief letter.

"Yeah, and for him to call her after 4:00 p.m. if he was interested. I would say that's rather suspicious." He checked the properties of the document. "She wrote it only a few days before Ryan Morgan's death." He swivelled in the chair to look up at Roberts.

"And now Tyler has gone missing from work. We have his home address. Shall we pay him a visit?"

"Let's a get a search warrant first. I'm thinking there may be reason to have a good look around his place."

———

ROBERTS AND STONE ARRIVED AT THE OLDER STUCCO EXTERIOR FOUR-PLEX. They parked at the front curb, looking at the patchy lawn trying to survive between two paved paths to the building. It appeared most people were content to take a short-cut across the grass rather than the sidewalk. A small wood sign proclaimed Harvest Apartments had no vacancy. In smaller lettering, it showed the building manager was in Unit B.

Stone led the way to the side of the building where Unit C was located. Past the detectives, an asphalt parking lot had two older vehicles parked, one looking like it hadn't moved in months.

Stone pressed the doorbell, waited a few seconds and pressed it again.

Roberts stated the obvious, "No answer."

"Not a surprise." Stone walked back to the front of the building. "Let's try the manager."

The pressing of the doorbell of Unit B resulted in the appearance of a pleasant looking woman of middle age. "How can I help you?"

Stone showed his identification. "We need to get inside Unit C. We do have a search warrant."

"Sure. I'll get you the key." A minute later, she returned with a brass key on a long chain. "I hope he's okay. He keeps to himself, pretty quiet renter."

Stone thanked her, returned to Unit B, and opened the door. A musty smell enveloped them.

"Kinda dark in here." Roberts flipped on the switch, revealing a small kitchen. Two empty pizza boxes sat on a sad looking table.

Stone entered the living room. A switch turned on a pole lamp. In the gloom, he saw a figure lying on a couch. On the floor was a syringe.

He rushed over, checking for vital signs. "Call 9-1-1!" Stone looked at Roberts. "He's still breathing."

Roberts quickly gave the information to the operator. "An ambulance will be here soon."

Stone nodded. "Damn." He looked at the prone man. "I had a buddy die of an overdose. What a fucked-up way to go."

"Nothing we can do right now." She placed a hand on his arm, remembering dark stories he told her over the years about his earlier life. His parents had died in a car accident when he was twenty. Later, he implied the accident occurred when both parents were either high or drunk. His older sister died from cancer. It left Stone troubled, often pushing the boundaries of what was safe. "I'll wait with him. Why don't you look around the kitchen and the rest of the house?"

He nodded and left the living room. He flipped on light switches, checking out the bedrooms, bathroom, and closets. There was little in the way of furniture or clothes. He looked under the bed, lifting the mattress to look underneath. He found a long-sleeved shirt lying in the bathroom. One end of a sleeve showed what appeared to dried blood splatters. He pushed the shirt into an evidence bag.

Stone used his flashlight in the closets, deciding nothing was hiding. An oversized closet with folding doors hid a washer and dryer. On top of the washer, a Phillips screwdriver rested.

"Firetruck is here."

Stone returned to the living room after hearing Roberts call out. The paramedic in a dark uniform informed them they would take over.

Roberts passed over her card. "It's important you let us know where you take him and if he regains consciousness."

"Will do."

Stone and Roberts watched them do their work, transfer the man to a stretcher and take him away.

"You okay?" Roberts asked Stone.

"Yeah. Thanks." He stared at the empty couch. "I've found nothing of hidden money so far, but I do have a shirt with what appears to be blood. Something for the lab. Let's go to the basement."

Roberts followed him and the flashlight beam down the stairs. The cool cement floor had only a few items. A bike, a few cardboard boxes, a bed frame and an open green toolbox.

Roberts and Stone found a string to pull that turned on a naked lightbulb. They examined the boxes, finding little of value. The toolboxes had an assortment of hand tools.

"No money hidden here," Stone remarked.

"There's still the kitchen." Roberts turned toward the stairs.

Stone pulled the string to turn off the light and met her in the kitchen. The cupboards contained various cans, boxes of cereal, pasta and seasonings, leaving half of the space empty. Stone opened the fridge, finding more beer than edible food. A pizza box with two slices took up one shelf. "A bachelor's diet."

Roberts opened the oven door. "Pretty clean in there. I suspect he's not much of a cook." She closed the door and opened the bottom drawer. A single baking sheet rested inside.

Stone looked around the countertops, seeing a couple of coffee cups, beer cans, and an empty plastic flask of vodka.

"I don't see anything," Roberts reported.

"Yeah, but..."

"What?" Roberts followed Stone as he returned to the hallway that led to the bedrooms. He stopped in front of the washer and dryer.

"What's this screwdriver doing here?"

"He was fixing something?" Roberts looked at the driver he was holding in his hand.

"But what? Nothing here but a washer and dryer. You can't fix one of those with only a screwdriver. He tugged out the dryer.

Roberts helped him position the dryer into the hallway. She unplugged the appliance. "Don't get yourself hurt."

"Ah, you do care about me." He removed the screws holding the rear plate of the dryer.

"No. It's just that I would have to explain to Cindy how you damaged yourself during an investigation. For reasons unknown, she cares about you."

"It's my charming personality." He removed the metal cover. "Bingo."

Roberts watched the money tumble to the floor. "Good guess on where the money was hidden."

"Good guess? Detective work in action."

"If you say so." She looked at the smug look on his face. "Alright, well done, Mr. Detective."

After taking several photographs, they placed the money, still wrapped in elastic bands, into evidence bags.

Roberts received a phone call from a paramedic, thanked him, and relayed the information to Stone. "Tyler Harris is recovering at the Royal Alec Hospital. He's still in rough shape, but will survive."

"Good, can you arrange to have the police guard him? We don't want him to disappear."

"Sure." She repeated his instructions on the phone. After she disconnected the call, she remarked, "You know, Moss, you can make these calls too. The only time I saw you use your phone was to order pickup for lunch."

"I'm conserving the phone battery."

"Hogwash. What's next? Paying Melisa Regan a visit?"

"You read my mind."

"That's a dangerous place to go."

———

MELISA REGAN GLARED AT THE DETECTIVES WHEN THEY STOOD AT HER door. "I'm tiring of your harassment. I've told you all I know, and I don't appreciate your interruptions of my time."

"Mind if we come in? If you want, we can wait until the search warrant arrives."

"Whatever." She stepped away from the door. "I'm calling my lawyer."

Stone and Roberts entered the apartment.

Stone heard Melisa talk on her phone, replying yes and okay several times.

"My lawyer will be here soon. She told me not to answer any questions, and since you don't have a search warrant yet, you can't look around."

"Fair enough." Stone sat on the couch. "Tell me, are you dating Tyler Harris?"

"Who?"

"Come on, he has your cell number. You have his home address. That sounds like a personal connection to me."

"I don't know what you're talking about."

"Yes, you do. Tyler Harris is under arrest. Do want him to confess first and throw you under the bus? Or do you want to get the jump on him and tell us what happened? Whoever talks first will probably get a favourable response from the prosecution."

"You can't prove anything."

"No? We can prove you know him. We can prove you were with him on the night of the murder. We can prove you had means, motive, and opportunity to murder Ryan Morgan. And if you don't think Tyler Harris won't confirm what happened on that Friday night, then you're in for a big shock."

"I think you should leave until my lawyer gets here."

"Ms. Regan, when we leave here, you'll be in cuffs."

"Fuck you." She sat in a chair and scowled at him.

A half hour passed slowly before the lawyer arrived. A tall woman with dark hair and a slim body stood in the centre of the room. "Helen Shaye. I'm Ms. Regan's attorney. Exactly what are the charges against my client?"

Stone stood. "Murder in the first degree."

"Impossible. Ms. Regan would never hurt anyone. She is often the victim of aggressive behaviour from men. If anything happened between her and a male client, it would have been in self-defence."

Stone looked at Roberts and back at the lawyer. "I don't know what you were told, but Melisa Regan conspired with a Tyler Harris to murder Ryan Morgan and steal monies in his safe. We have Tyler Harris in custody. We have his share of the stolen money. I don't care if Harris or your client confesses first. But both are going to prison. How long she spends behind bars depends on a lot if she stays silent or tells us exactly what happened. Your move."

"I want to talk privately with Melisa." Shaye went with her to a bedroom.

Roberts looked at Stone. "Think she'll confess?"

"I think she'll put the blame on Harris, and that she was only there when it happened."

"She's one wicked woman."

"I tend to agree."

Helen Shaye returned. "We would like to make a statement. Ryan Morgan was known for his wealth and womanizing. Melisa was having an affair with him when she discovered he was having a second affair. She broke up with him, and enlisted an acquaintance of hers, Tyler Harris, to accompany her. My client was concerned about Ryan Morgan's temper and feared for her safety when he was told of her decision to break it off with him.

"When they arrived at his office, Ryan Morgan was dying from stab wounds. Melisa wanted to call for help, but Harris became aggressive and used a knife to slice his throat. He then took monies from an open safe. Tyler Harris threatened Melisa if she said anything, he would kill her as well.

"My client has nothing to do with the murder of Ryan Morgan, and in fact, wanted to save his life. Ms. Regan is a victim in this terrible episode as well."

Stone shook his head. "Wow. That is quite the fanciful tale. I rather doubt Tyle Harris will say that's what happened."

"What do you expect? Tyler Harris is a murderer. You can't believe anything he says."

"And I'm supposed to believe what she says? Sorry, it doesn't work that way. But, by her own admission, she was present during the murder of Ryan Morgan. Therefore, I'm charging your client as an accomplice to murder." He held up a pair of handcuffs. "I told you, you'll be leaving in cuffs."

———

STONE AND ROBERTS TOOK MELISA REGAN TO THE STREET LEVEL, WHERE A waiting police car took her away. They returned to her apartment, where the lawyer was still waiting.

"You have a warrant to a search here?"

"Yup. Please don't get in our way." Stone handed her a folded document.

"You won't find anything."

"Why are you so certain?"

"I know Melisa Regan." She frowned.

Stone raised his eyebrows. "I'm not sure if that's really an endorsement." He looked at Roberts. "Why don't you look in the bedrooms? I'll investigate the kitchen and bar."

Stone went into the kitchen, opening cupboard doors, the refrigerator, and the oven. He moved the neighbouring bar, checking the various spirits and the inside of the wine fridge.

"You see, nothing." Helen Shaye spoke.

Stone ignored her. He looked around the living room, lifting chair cushions, moving tables and tapping walls for signs of a hidden access. He stopped in the centre of the room, looking at the paintings on the walls. He smiled.

Roberts entered the living room. "No hidden money or knives. But I found this in one of the drawers." She held up paper with numbers and letters typed across.

"Interesting. Perhaps an offshore banking account or a password to digital currency."

"What did you find?" Roberts asked.

Stone looked at Shaye and back to Roberts. "I believe I figured how she converted her cash to a commodity." He went over to a wall and lifted a painting off the hanger. "I saw photos of Melisa earlier on the computer. What she had on the walls were prints. These are originals." He turned the painting around to look at the back and peeled off an envelope taped to underside. "A certificate of authenticity." He spoke to Roberts. "I'll bet she purchased this painting recently with cash. There's another painting on the opposite wall." He looked at the lawyer. "I guess we found something."

"I'll converse with you later on this." Shaye hurried out of the room.

Stone looked at Roberts. "It looks like we struck a nerve."

33

Thursday Evening

STONE AND ROBERTS ENTERED THE SEMI-PRIVATE ROOM AT THE ROYAL Alec Hospital. A cop stood by the door.

"Semi-private?" Stone asked the cop.

"Bed shortage. I was told to take it up with the government."

Stone saw a scruffy-looking man resting in a bed with one wrist handcuffed to the bed frame. He showed him his badge. "How are you feeling?"

"Not good. I don't even know how I got here."

"Your good fortune we were investigating the murder of Ryan Morgan and found you passed out from a drug overdose." Stone waited as he absorbed the information. "We believe you murdered our victim, along with Melisa Regan. You stole the money in the safe. Spent some on drugs, and now here you are."

"Oh."

"Do You understand what we just told you? You're being accused of murder."

"Uh, yeah. What happens next?"

Stone looked at Roberts. "You have a right to a lawyer. Do you want one?"

"I think so. Sorry. I can't think straight right now."

"Okay, we'll talk later."

Stone left with Roberts. "If he had confessed, it might be thrown out of court due to his state of mind. It's best we wait until his brain is working properly."

"Okay, let's go to the office and see what we got for evidence."

————

STONE DRANK A CUP OF COFFEE AS HE SAT AT HIS DESK. "WHAT DID WE find out about the paintings?"

"By we, I presume you mean me. You were right. She purchased the paintings on the Saturday after the murder. They were delivered right away from Northern Art Impressions. I talked to them on the phone, and they admit selling and delivering the art pieces to her. Very expensive, original artwork. She paid with a money order."

"She got rid of the cash rather quickly."

"She did. The numbers I found were for a bank account in the Cayman Islands. I'm under the impression that Melisa Regan is used to hiding cash from authorities. Her activity as an escort would mean she prefers cash and then has a means to put it where the government can't find it."

"Makes sense. Her job as office manager with Morgan would show the government, she does a small taxable income. And working with Morgan would allow her to meet other wealthy men who would enjoy paying for her services."

"Okay, let's review what we do know, or suspect what happened." Roberts held up a finger. "One, Ryan Morgan has given cause to a number of people who would like to see him dead. Two, Joseph McCarthy pretended to spend time in the gym, but instead knifed Morgan in the back, leaving him to die. Three, Melisa and her accomplice Tyler Harris find Ryan Morgan dying. They finish him off and steal the money from the safe."

"Now all we need is confessions."

Roberts looked at her monitor. "I have a message from the lab." She hit a few keys on her keyboard and read the text. "We have a match. The blood on the shirt you found is a match for Ryan Morgan. That will make it easier to seek a confession from Harris."

"Great, let's get the ball rolling. It's time to chat with Tyler Harris and his lawyer."

34

September 1, Friday Morning

STONE TAPPED A FEW KEYS AS SHE LOOKED AT HIS COMPUTER MONITOR. "IT seems our boy, Tyler Harris, was a bright lad. He completed his bachelor's in science. Then it seems he hit hard times. His employment history is scattered to odd jobs."

"Well, murder would be a new low for him." Roberts peered over his shoulder. "Tyler Harris is now available for an interview. Let's bring him from the holding cell and have a conversation with him. We better make sure his court-appointed lawyer is here as well."

Stone walked to the coffee room, getting another cup for himself. By the time he arrived at the interview room, Roberts was sitting across from Tyler Harris. Harris looked tired as he slouched in his chair, a bottle of water was opened in front of him. His face, with a scruffy beard, was without expression. Standing next to Harris was a nervous looking young man.

"You must be his attorney." Stone looked up at the standing man.

"Yes, Nigel Oliver." He pushed a business card across the table.

"Good to meet you. Why don't you have a seat?" Stone waited until the lawyer sat and opened a folder. "Mr. Harris, we have a situation of a murdered man and the contents of his safe stolen. We found the stolen money hidden in your apartment, and the victim's blood on your shirt. Anything you'd to say about that?"

Harris stirred and attempted to sit up straight.

"How do you know it was the victim's blood, and the money was stolen?" Oliver asked.

"The money and the shirt were found in his apartment. Our lab confirmed the blood on the shirt to match Ryan Morgan. The money matched the description of what was placed in the safe earlier. Unless Mr. Harris has an invisible roommate, I would say he is guilty of murder and robbery."

"Did you have a search warrant?"

"We did. Does your client have anything to say in his defence?" Stone flipped open a page inside the folder in front of him. "Does this photo ring any bells?" He slid across a photo of Ryan Morgan lying dead in a pool of blood around his head.

Harris jerked in his chair and wiped a hand across his head. "Shit."

"I advise you not to say anything right now," Oliver quickly spoke.

"Look, man, I didn't go there to kill him. She said we could just take money out of the safe, that she knew the combination."

"What happened when you arrived there? Who is she?"

"Don't speak."

Harris looked around and licked his lips. "I was high, you know, spaced out. I went with that bitch, Melisa. She said it was easy money. I didn't know he would be there."

"Did you kill Ryan Morgan?"

"She screamed at me to finish him off. Just kept yelling at me."

"Look, my client obviously was on drugs at the time of the murder. He lacked capacity for what was happening."

"I want to confess. I'm having nightmares." Harris pushed the photo away.

"Can I have a few minutes alone with my client?"

Stone stood. "Sure. Just so you know, we also have Melisa Regan in custody. She may claim it was all Tyler's idea, and she was forced to go along. Don't wait too long to tell his side of the story."

Roberts and Stone left the interview room.

"Do you think he'll confess?" Roberts asked as they stood by the closed door of the interview room.

"I do, unless that brand new lawyer talks him out of it." Stone took a drink of his coffee. "I don't want to screw this up. I don't want either Harris or Regan to escape on a technicality or missing evidence. So far, it looks like Joseph McCarthy has gotten away with his attack on Morgan."

Oliver opened the door. "Mr. Harris would like to make a statement." He didn't look pleased.

Stone and Roberts sat again at the table, facing Harris.

"How about we start when you received a letter from Melisa Regan," Stone initiated the interview.

"Yeah, sure. I got this envelope couriered to me. It said if I wanted to make some quick money to call her. I did. She told me there was money in a safe where she worked and she knew the combination number. She wanted someone to help her carry out the cash.

"Then on the day we were to get together, she told me to bring a gun or knife, just in case someone came along. I carry a knife with me a lot. You know, I buy and sell drugs. It's good to have a weapon."

"Okay, after she told you to bring a weapon, you still went ahead with the robbery."

"Yeah, well, I was pretty high then. I wasn't thinking straight."

"Where did you meet her?"

"The coffee shop across from his office." Harris shifted in his seat, taking a drink from his bottle of water.

"So you went up to his office together?" Stone stared at his empty cup and sighed.

Harris nodded. "We got to his office and went inside this second office. That's when I saw this guy trying to crawl on the floor. He looked up and asked for help."

"But you didn't help him," Roberts interjected.

"She kept yelling at me to kill him. I don't why I did, but I used my knife to slice his throat." He covered his face with his hands. "Fuck me."

He shook his head. "I just kept hearing her scream, kill him, kill him. So I did."

"Then what?" Roberts asked.

"We split the money from the safe. I went home, changed, and went to work at the bar."

"You went to work after that?" Stone asked.

"I was still strung out. It didn't occur to me not to go to work. After my shift, I went home, hid the money inside the dryer. I fell asleep. When I woke up, I went out and bought more drugs. Then I passed out."

Roberts looked at her notes. "What happened, Tyler? You went to university, got your bachelor of science. Now this?"

"It started during my final year. I broke a leg during a soccer game. I got hooked on painkillers. I really screwed up my life. I'm sorry for what I did. But that bitch, she ain't sorry."

"Thank you for your cooperation, Mr. Harris." Stone stood. "I'll make sure the court knows of your willingness to confess."

Stone walked with Roberts to the coffee room. "Now we have a confession from Harris, let's see what Ms. Regan has to say."

"I suspect her story may differ." Roberts added milk to her own coffee.

"Let's take a break and have her called up to the interview room. Let's contact her lawyer. No point in trying to get her to say anything without her council present."

35

Friday Afternoon

A POLICE OFFICER ESCORTED MELISA REGAN TO THE INTERVIEW. Following was attorney Helen Shaye, who sat next to her.

Stone waited for Roberts to sit first, and then sat next to her. He opened a folder. "Do you want to give your version of the events on the night of Ryan Morgan's death? Or would you prefer to hear from us on how you conspired to commit murder and robbery?"

"My client is innocent of any and all charges. It is up to you to prove she had anything to do with the most unfortunate death of her employer and friend, Mr. Morgan. She is still grieving for his loss."

"Really? It would impress Walt Disney with that fantasy tale." Stone tapped his pen on the table. "Why don't you tell me what happened, Ms. Regan, let's say, after you found out Ryan Morgan was having an affair not only with you but also with another woman?"

Regan took a deep breath. "I don't know what you're talking about."

"Of course you do. But how about we ask an easier question? Tell us when you met Tyler Harris at Charmaine's Coffee Emporium, and then went to Ryan Morgan's office."

"Tyler approached me to split the contents of the safe in Ryan Morgan's office. He said he would provide the muscle, if there was any trouble, if I could open the safe."

"Nice arrangement. What is the combination of the safe?"

"I, I, I don't know it off-hand. I wrote it down somewhere."

"Where? Tell us so we can verify the numbers," Stone questioned her.

"I can't remember right now."

"Alright. You now leave the coffee shop with Harris and go to Morgan's office. What happened after you left the elevator on his office floor?"

Regan took a deep breath. "We went to his office and opened the door..."

"It was unlocked?"

"Yes. We went inside and into Ryan's private office. It shocked me to see him on the floor, badly hurt. Before I could react, Tyler used his knife to slice his throat. I was scared. It was brutal. It paralyzed me with fear.

"Then Tyler ordered me to open the safe, which I did."

"The safe was already unlocked?"

"Yes."

"You split the monies?"

"Yes."

"Then what?"

"I can't remember. It was a blur to me. I went home and cried. I was so upset at Ryan's death."

"Yet we contacted you the next day. You claim you couldn't see us because you had an appointment. You didn't appear to be distraught when we saw you on Sunday."

"They gave me medication to help me cope with the tragedy. I wasn't feeling myself."

Stone looked at his notes. "Let's take a step back. When Harris and you first saw Ryan Morgan in the office, did you say anything to Harris?"

"No."

"You didn't tell him to kill Morgan?"

"No, I was too scared to speak."

Stone rubbed his eyes. "I truly hate dealing with liars, especially the ones that only care for themselves."

"I wasn't lying."

"If you think accusing my client of lying, without proof, will help you to solve this case, I assure you I can make your head spin with official complaints." Helen Shaye glared at Stone.

"We solved the murder. I just need to put the guilty parties into jail." He pointed a finger at Regan. "That most certainly includes you." He tapped his pen on the table. "Okay, here is what we know. You contacted Tyler Harris to rob Ryan Morgan's safe. By your own admission, when we talked to you the following Sunday, you knew Ryan Morgan worked late. That's why you returned that Friday evening. You didn't know the safe combination and if he was there, then the safe wasn't locked. If it was locked, you could force him to open the safe."

"That is preposterous," Shaye retorted.

"Morgan's gun, the one he kept in his desk for protection, was empty of bullets. Your client's fingerprints are on the gun. She emptied the gun of bullets to ensure Morgan couldn't easily defend himself. Does Ms. Regan wish to deny she removed the bullets from his gun?"

Shaye looked at Regan.

"Yes, I did. It was because Ryan was prone to moments of anger. I removed the bullets so he couldn't use it against me."

"You just keep pushing the boundaries of credibility further each time." Stone crossed his arms. "I have all the information I require from the confession of Tyler Harris. Ms. Regan, either you tell us the truth right now and confess to accessory to the murder of Ryan Morgan, or we will proceed with conspiracy to commit murder, fraud and armed robbery. If we proceed with robbery, we will notify Revenue Canada of your hidden assets. I will give you precisely four minutes to decide." He stood. "Three minutes and fifty seconds." He stepped out of the interview room with Roberts.

"That was a bit of a bluff. We didn't know for sure it was her fingerprints on the gun." She stood with Stone by the closed door.

"We do now."

"Do you think she'll confess?"

"She doesn't know what we actually know." Stone looked at the interview room. "I think she values keeping her money. If she refuses to confess, she'll risk losing her assets."

"Won't Revenue Canada go after the money, anyway?"

"Yeah, well, she doesn't know that." He looked at his watch. "Five minutes. Let's go in."

Helen Shaye looked up when they entered. "We acknowledged Melisa was caught up in events of which she had little control. Therefore, she will admit to being an accessory to Tyler Harris in the murder of Ryan Morgan. We do not admit to being the main party, or instigator, of the murder and subsequent robbery."

"Fair enough. We'll take her statement. But and I'll warn you just this once, any lies, or misleading information, in your statement means all bets are off. Be smart and give us the entire story," Stone warned her.

Regan nodded.

"We'll have someone type out your statement." Roberts signalled for a cop to enter the room. "Watch her while we get someone to take her statement."

"Let's go. I need a coffee." Stone walked out of the room.

Roberts walked with him to the coffee room. "Okay, we have confessions from Tyler Harris and Melisa Regan. Anything else with this murder we need to do?"

"Yup. I want to push Joseph McCarthy for a confession. I'm certain he stabbed Morgan in the back. I want him to confess to it."

"Shall we interview him at his home or have him brought in here?"

"Here. Let's get him out of his comfort zone."

"Okay. I'll have him brought into our office. Tomorrow morning good?"

"Yup. Call him today and let him know. Let's see how well he sleeps knowing he'll be coming downtown in the morning."

36

Saturday Morning

"RACHEL MCCARTHY INSISTED ON ARRIVING WITH HER HUSBAND." Roberts pointed at the woman standing outside the interview room. "And do you remember the lawyer, Levi Hurley? He's here as well. It seems Michael Sutton recommended him to Joseph."

"Great," Stone replied sarcastically. "Let's get this show going." He walked to the interview room, carrying a fresh cup of coffee.

Stone closed the door of the interview room, leaving Rachel McCarthy standing outside, her arms crossed as she peered at the frosted glass windows.

Hurley spoke first. "I've advised my client he does not need to say a single word. I believe you have asked him here in nothing more than a fishing expedition. Unless you have new, specific evidence that he may have committed a crime, I believe this interview is over."

"I admire you for liking to come to the point, Mr. Hurley," Stone replied. "So, I shall do the same. A few days ago, when we informed Mr. McCarthy that the perpetrator who stabbed Ryan Morgan in the back did not kill him, but merely injured him, it caused quite a reaction with him. I know facial expressions, and I know that Joseph McCarthy attacked Ryan Morgan and left him for dead." He looked at McCarthy's face, saw the flushed expression and the slack jaw.

"Can you prove it?" Hurley challenged.

"Right now, no. We have focused our efforts on the actual killers of Ryan Morgan. Now that we have them in custody, I can start working on finding proof you lied being at the gym. Do you know how many traffic cameras are in the city? How many security cameras along the roads that may have captured your vehicle going by? How about if I interview every person in the gym that night to see if any of them remember you leaving early? How confident do you feel I won't find just one clue that destroys your alibi?"

"But you have nothing yet. I'm still advising my client not to say anything to you."

Stone clicked his pen a few times.

"Detective Stone, I don't believe you'll ever find anything that will contradict what I've told you." McCarthy ignored Hurley's hand signal to be quiet. "However, let's put it this way. Let's say you went to see Ryan about an affair he had with your wife and has photos of her in a compromising position. You go to his office, and you have a knife, but aren't sure if you need to use it. When you try to talk to him, he tells you to scram, that you're a wimp.

"You see his phone on the desk, and you grab it. Ryan struggles to get it back from you, calling you an idiot. That's when you strike him. He falls to the floor, and you smash his cellphone. You're ready to leave. You've done what you came to do. But he gets up on his hands and knees, sees his broken phone, and calls your wife a whore and a slut. That's when you make use of the knife."

Stone nodded. "Are you saying you weren't planning to murder Ryan Morgan?"

"No, I'm saying *you* weren't planning to murder him."

Hurley interjected. "In no way was this an admission of guilt. It was a what-if story."

"It sounded like more than a story to me." Stone scribbled in notebook. "Any more to this story you want to tell?"

McCarthy shook his head. "That's all I have to say."

"Are we done here?" Hurley asked.

"Yup. Thanks for coming in."

Stone watched McCarthy hug his wife.

Hurley paused at the exit of the interview room. "You have nothing on him. That was a bit of bullshit on checking video cameras." He gave a smile. "Nice try, though."

Roberts approached Stone. "So, is that the end of trying to convict Joseph McCarthy?"

"Yeah. If Ryan Morgan was stupid enough to insult McCarthy's wife while he was holding knife... Let's just say that was really dumb."

"Are we going to let Brooke Morgan know about McCarthy's assault? I assume we'll go there to let her know that we have captured her killers."

"I don't see the point in telling her about our speculation on Joseph McCarthy. It would not make her feel any better that a friend of hers tried to kill her husband. If the truth doesn't serve a purpose, perhaps it best be left unspoken."

———

BROOKE MORGAN OPENED THE FRONT DOOR, GIVING THEM A SOFT SMILE. "Come in, detectives. We were just having drinks."

They followed her past the living room and kitchen to the patio. Sitting at a table, he saw Paige Butler and Michael Sutton.

"Wine?"

"Sure." Stone saw the surprised look on her face. "One won't hurt. I'm not here to accuse anyone of a crime."

Stone and Roberts sat, exchanging greetings with Paige and Michael.

Brooke went back to the kitchen and returned with two glasses. She poured the white wine. "Sauvignon Blanc from France."

Stone sniffed the wine glass. "Nice." He saw the label on the bottle.

"Chateau Camarsac. I'll have to remember that name. I might impress my girlfriend by buying a bottle for her."

Brooke laughed. "Trying to make your girlfriend happy by giving her wine? That may work."

Stone took a sip of the wine. "I like this." He looked over at Roberts.

"Thank you for the wine. Detective Stone and I have concluded our investigation of the murder of your husband."

Brooke froze in position, her wineglass on her lap as she sat at the table.

"Two people were involved. One was Melisa Regan, his office manager. The other was Tyler Harris, a worker at the Hi-Lite Bar. Their motive for murder was money held in the safe of his office." Roberts took a drink of her wine.

"I see. No one else was involved?"

"We don't have any evidence of a third person," Stone replied. He noticed Michael slowly release his breath.

Brooke nodded. "Thank you so much for bringing closure. It was dreadful not knowing who could have done this to him."

Stone and Roberts finished their wine and stood.

"Ms. Butler, I have a knife that belongs to you in the car," Stone spoke to her.

Butler stood. "I'll be right back."

Stone walked with Stone and Roberts to his car. "Thanks for not implying there wasn't anyone else involved in the murder. Michael was worried you would say something."

Stone opened his trunk, retrieving a clear bag holding a knife. "Here you go." He reached into his coat pocket and passed her a flash drive. "Your photos."

"Thank you. You know, you kind of grow on a person. You have a prickly exterior, but you're a decent person underneath."

"I'll take that as a compliment. Is your triangle complete again?"

She grinned. "Yes. Michael and Brooke are soulmates. I suspect they will announce an engagement soon."

Stone and Roberts got into the car. As Stone drove down the street, he looked over at Roberts. "There's something to be said for what Michael, Paige and Brooke have. Close friends are hard to beat."

"That's true."

"So thanks for being my friend and partner."

"Back at you."

————

Don't miss out on your next favorite book!

Join the Melange Books mailing list at
www.melange-books.com/mail.html

THANK YOU FOR READING

Did you enjoy this book?

We invite you to leave a review at the website of your choice, such as Goodreads, Amazon, Barnes & Noble, etc.

DID YOU KNOW THAT LEAVING A REVIEW...

- Helps other readers find books they may enjoy.
- Gives you a chance to let your voice be heard.
- Gives authors recognition for their hard work.
- Doesn't have to be long. A sentence or two about why you liked the book will do.

ABOUT THE AUTHOR

Jack Wear started his writing career over fifteen years ago. After he left the employ of Xerox as a service technician, he decided on a new occupation of selling wine. During that time, he began to write, and two years later sold his first book to a publisher. Perhaps the initial success was due to selling of wine, as the two seem to go well together. In fact, one of his murder mysteries occurred at a wine festival.

Jack's interests are varied, showing a passion for astronomy, physics, photography and wine. His writing shows that varied interest. He writes in several genres, including science fiction, fantasy and murder mysteries. He feels fortunate his publisher, Melange Books, accepts his interest in writing diverse categories.

Jack was born and raised in Edmonton, resisting the temptation to live in warmer climates by convincing himself he loves snow. He is married and has three sons and two grandsons.

www.jhwear.com

 twitter.com/JH_Wear

ALSO BY JH WEAR

Novels

Witches and Warriors

Shadows And Sensations

Dragons in the Water

A Taste Of Murder

A Hole in the Universe

Play Dead

Back Stabber

———

Castle Series

#1 Fall to Domum

#2 The Curse of the Dacron Gem

#3 The New King

www.ingramcontent.com/pod-product-compliance
Lightning Source LLC
Chambersburg PA
CBHW020602250626
47154CB00004B/1330